The B.I.T.N. Bureau Assignments

Welcome to Dunhope Manor

KATHERINE DEMPSTER

WELCOME TO DUNHOPE MANOR

The B.I.T.N. Bureau Assignments
Book Two

Katherine Dempster

Dedicated to anyone who believed themselves trapped until they found their wings and soared.

CHAPTER ONE

X
WHEEL of FORTUNE.

If there was one thing that Nora had come to understand, it was that there is more than one type of prison. Not all are cold, barren cells holding you in place by inescapable steel bars. Some prisons were beautiful to everyone but the prisoner. Opulent homes filled with the trappings of wealth, surrounded by cruel and loveless families. Much like the one she had grown up in and escaped to Aumbry Valley from. As bad as her memories of that time were, she now knew that the most destructive prison held absolute power just by residing in your head. The hate and sorrow of the past that had haunted her new friend Ezra was an example of that torture. The prison of one's mind is the most powerful and constrictive of all possibilities. Nora's current prison was a rundown old manor home in the tiny valley town that she was powerless to leave. Seeing Ezra overcome the paralyzing prison of his mind within those walls was a constant reminder that things could be so much worse.

Her actual surroundings had significantly improved over the past couple of months, thanks to moving from her tiny shell of a studio-sized space on the first floor of Dunhope Manor into a much larger one-bedroom apartment on the third floor. Ezra's home, a few streets over that he had been renovating, was graciously purchased by The Firm when it was decided that the threats that had been creeping around in the shadows had become more focused on the two of them. He had tried to dig his heels in and remain in his home, even suggesting that Nora move into the house with him when they were told they were to be kept close with a constant presence of security.

Without further discussion, he had been ushered over to the manor to take up residence in a sun-drenched apartment on the second floor. Nora plunging a stake into Jude's back had been an appreciated end to the threat he posed to the BITN Bureau, and that horrifying moment put them all in her debt. Unfortunately, that needed to be cashed in sooner rather than later when word reached them of Quinn's desire to avenge his death. The manor's walls were the only thin layer of protection they had between them and a deranged, vengeful vampire who used to be Nora's best friend, her only aunt. The building itself was reinforced by all the might of her friend and landlady Jenny and the coven she had revealed herself to be a part of. It seemed wrong to bring Jenny and her sweet three-year-old daughter, Olivia, into such a dangerous situation. That the building was ironically originally built by Jude decades ago before he was made vampire. Now that Jenny owned it, the kind, young witch did not blink twice about protecting it and its few occupants. Nora's neighbor Norman, an anxiety-filled shut-in with a friendly yet shy smile, and Ezra's neighbor, Gail, an older woman with a penchant for caring for her beloved songbirds, did not seem to realize who and what they were sharing a roof with. Nora felt guilt when she caught a glimpse of her neighbors and sent up silent prayers that the danger that the universe had brought to her life would stay clear of them.

Jenny was happy to assist with the protection and care of Nora and Ezra and was also grateful for the extra rent money. Ezra's handy work was also a blessing as he started bringing the manor back to life with his many renovation skills. It was a double blessing that puttering with repairs kept his mind occupied and calm while he was locked down within those walls. Jude was visible to her in every corner of the previously decadent home, and Ezra was happy to remove any trace of him. As the decades of grime were slowly chipped away, each wall and floorboard sang out with a history that seemed more beautiful than the truth the walls held.

The B.I.T.N crew had taken over her first little apartment as a headquarters of sorts to keep tabs on the two ever since they were put on lockdown within the building, having at least three of them on duty twenty-four/seven. Having the largest of the apartments now, Nora's place had become the communal hangout during the day for some of the crew, along with Jenny and Ezra. They had all melted into a routine that had the appearance of normality. One of the most significant changes to her day-to-day life was that Ezra had started to spend more time in her apartment than in his own. Being used to a solitary life, it was strange for Nora at first. Slowly, over the past few months, the apartment felt too large and lonely when he would make his way down to his own space after everyone else had left to live their own lives and see to their day-to-day duties.

"Can you make those little noodles again?" Ezra asked, tossing himself onto Nora's couch.

"Why don't you make them? It's just boiling water and heating up the sauce," Nora asked, picking up her cat Silas' bowl to refill it with his dinner. The large grey fur ball was quite content with the extra room to stretch and sunbathe. Not to mention having Nora home almost constantly to indulge his every whim.

"Hey now, I carried the groceries all the way up three flights of stairs. I think I should get a meal or two for that effort," Ezra moaned, stretching out. Nora tried to ignore the peek of his lean stomach that appeared below the edge of his shirt. She spent much time trying to ignore the little details of him that were making themselves apparent. Being cooped up together was playing with her mind. There is something about being in close quarters with someone that pushes your feelings further in one direction or the other, and she would shake off the little moments that had her taking a second look at him. Luckily, the emotions were primarily positive other than playful teasing. Ezra had become like a brother to her, and they fought like they were actually siblings. It felt silly to let her mind wander to ideas of a man whom she was sure thought of her as a little sister. It's not like she had a lot of options being locked up, and she told herself it was not a situation that would last forever. She had to believe that she would be free of the mess created by Quinn, or she wouldn't be able to get out of bed in the morning.

"Poor baby is working himself to the bone," Nora teased.

"*Poor baby* is going stir-crazy in this damn house all the time. It's been months, and nothing has happened. If they don't start telling us what's going on with those disgusting blood-suckers, I'm going to lose it completely," Ezra fumed, rolling onto his side and turning on Nora's newly purchased television.

The screen was too big for the space, although they didn't mind. Elijah had taken advantage of his position in the bureau and allowed them to purchase anything they wanted to make themselves comfortable. Nora had mistakenly asked Gabriel to get them a new television. She should have known that the extravagant and eccentric vampire would go overboard. The spells the coven worked made it impossible for Gabriel to enter the building, which was well enough now that Ezra was unfriendly to the exuberantly entertaining man simply because he was a vampire. Nora tried to reason with Ezra that it was Gabriel's help that had saved them when Jude and Quinn had their cult-like followers attack his house in an attempt to drag them out. Ezra was steadfast that a vampire was a vampire first above all else and, therefore, an enemy. She could tell that Gabriel noticed that he was being cold to him when he called or during a rare visit to the window to check in on them, but in classic Gabriel style, he played it off with humor.

The vampire took to making peace with gifts. Nora made sure to point out every time Ezra enjoyed one. The massive television was one that Ezra could not bring himself to turn his back on. It had become their only glimpse into the world they once lived in before Aumbry Valley and Dunhope Manor. Lately, it had been silly reality shows about beautiful drunk twenty-somethings that Nora was surprised to find Ezra sucked into. Not relatable but definitely mind-numbing, and that is just what the doctor ordered in their current situation.

"I don't think you're going to find any breaking news about vampires on there, Ez."

"Whatever. It kills time, and that's good enough," he mumbled, clicking the remote through the viewing options.

Ezra's hate for vampires was understandable, and it seemed cruel to force him to live in what had been Jude's house before he had been turned. Jude had destroyed his family and a large portion of his heart, and he was now trapped within the walls of the murderer's home until Quinn was found and the threat to them was eliminated. Nora hated when they used that word. No matter what Quinn had become or done, she was still Nora's family. There had to be a trace of shared blood left in her, and to think of her being *eliminated* hurt.

Three rapid knocks on the door echoed through the apartment. The sound was the distinct announcement of Rowan's arrival. Nora was happy to have him on the crew in charge of the building's security. Not just because he was gorgeous; he was always upbeat and seemed to be damn good at his job. Nora unlocked the heavy, newly installed silver locks and opened the door wide with a grin to let him in. The feelings that were growing for Ezra felt awkward, but when it came to Rowan Andries, Nora was happy to exchange a flirt here and there. His tall, broad, golden-boy looks gave him the appearance of one of the fae Glamour Guards she had encountered in Elijah's office. It was hard to believe he was just a plain old human like her. Well, not exactly plain.

"Hey, Rowan! How's your day been? Any crazy vampires scratching at the door?" Nora asked, squirming with embarrassment at how excited she sounded. She tried to push her broad grin into a less obvious size, tightening her lips.

"Nope, no day walkers out to get you today," he replied with a laugh and a nod of hello to Ezra.

"Day...there aren't really...," Nora waited for the information on vampires to spring to her mind. The Ascension she had been given at the beginning of her indoctrination into the world of supernaturals had given them an encyclopedia of information planted in her head. Answers to questions she would think of would pop out from time to time. It was not much of a surprise when nothing came to mind. Most of the benefits of the fae blood she was given had started to weaken by the day. Her reflexes and speed were slowing down as much as her inability to pull the knowledge out.

"No, there's not, Nora," Rowan smiled down at her, "As far as I know, I guess. I'm not surprised by much anymore," he added, walking into the apartment. He tapped at Ezra's feet to get him to make room for him to sit, "Like this guy sprawled out on your couch."

"What? Her place is nicer," Ezra blustered, sitting up quickly and switching off the television.

"I guess it has come along from the dust trap that it was. Not a bad trade for almost being vamp food," Rowan jested, looking around the newly decorated space.

"Funny. You're a funny guy, Rowan," Nora shook her head at him.

He gave a smirk and a shrug of his shoulders, "Speaking of vamps...."

"Aren't we always talking about them?" Ezra interrupted and pulled himself up from the couch to go forage in Nora's fridge.

It was true that very little had been discussed since "The Night," which is what they had taken to calling the evening of Jude's death. It was no wonder Ezra spent his days keeping his hands busy or mind-melding with the TV.

"I guess it goes with the job," Rowan said with a friendly chuckle.

"I wouldn't call being held captive a job, so why are we always talking about them," Ezra snapped, slamming the fridge closed.

He was edgier than usual. Nora watched him glare at Rowan and frowned. It wasn't fair to snap at someone who was only trying to keep them safe.

"Well, I mean...you are getting paid pretty well," Rowan said in an apparent attempt to break the tension. The snort from Ezra let him know that it wasn't appreciated. "So, anyway," he turned to Nora, "Elijah said he'll be by in the morning for an update. I don't want to jump the gun and say it's good news, but there has been a lot of chatter that says it will be."

Nora's stomach twisted. Every mention of Quinn made her head spin with emotions. Betrayal, worry, guilt, and happiness. Whatever the ending to Quinn's battle would be was never far from Nora's thoughts. Even though she had been told that particular sentence was rarely given, there was an order to stake on sight. The full details of the damage Jude and Quinn had caused were not offered to Nora, no matter how many times she asked. If the fae thought the vampires were low on the food chain, mortals were even lower. It was not even on the table to share details of the supernatural world and the battles within with someone who had been merely bait. In return, they were protecting her from the fallout and nothing more. What she did know is that Jude had caused enough of an uprising, including moles inside The Firm, that the fae were worried enough to threaten to destroy the body of The Maker that they had protected within their vaults. That would mean the end of all vampires. It was a threat they gave and withdrew within hours. It made Nora look at the idea of immortality a little differently and avoid the fae at all costs. They did not live within the moral concepts that mortals attempted to do. The fairies were as cold as they were beautiful.

"Did they find her?" Nora asked softly.

"I can't say for sure. From what I'm hearing, there is a chance that the group that was attempting the coup fell apart pretty quickly when everyone left the valley. It seems Jude's reach wasn't as far as he had everyone believing, so once he, you know...."

"Got staked straight down to hell by Nora," Ezra finished, interrupting Rowan once more, "and the world owes her a thank you for it."

Nora glowered at him. She wasn't as keen on the fact that she had taken a life as he was, even if he was a murdering vampire that had turned her aunt against her. The embers and ash that enveloped her hand around the broken spindle she had plunged into his back still swirled in her nightmares.

"Yeah, when *that* happened, things started to fall apart. Having a newbie vampire with a stake on sight warrant on her head doesn't really bring a lot of faith to the followers," Rowan said flatly.

"Does it look like we'll be able to leave soon? At least leave the building?" Nora asked, her eyes wide with hope. She would go mad if she didn't focus on the small positives. Leaving Aumbry Valley behind and forgetting it ever existed was the current fantasy she repeated to herself in the darkness of her bedroom to drown the terror her dreams would bring.

"I don't know. When it comes down to it, you both took the life of immortals, and there was no punishment from the Council. Vampires won't take lightly to that whether they agreed with Jude or not. It could still be dangerous out there for both of you," Rowan frowned when he saw the sigh of disappointment slip from Nora, "Like I said, I don't know much more than that. Elijah will give you the details. I'm heading out now and will be back in the morning. Hopefully, we'll all know more then," Rowan gave a look of well-intended pity and headed for the door, "I just wanted to check in and give you the heads up."

"Did you want to stay for dinner? We're just doing pasta, nothing fancy," Nora offered, hoping he would stay.

"No, I'm good. Thanks though. I need to update the night crew before I leave, and I still have to check in at Elijah's office before heading home. Gabriel has news for us, apparently," he twisted the row of locks open and opened the door.

"If you only get a few hours off every night, you may as well sleep here and be trapped in these walls twenty-four-seven like us," Ezra suggested with a bitter laugh.

"I would, but it looks like the couch is taken already," Rowan grinned with a wink.

Ezra looked quickly between the two, his face tight, "I meant down in the HQ," he cleared his throat, "I told you, this place is just more comfortable, okay? My apartment is always filled with the squawking of Gail's damn birds, and that's when she's not trapping me in the hallway to talk my ear off. Her lips flap more than the yappy birds' wings."

"I'm glad I can't hear them up here. That would be so annoying," Nora added to try to break the tense glare between the two. Even Rowan had started to get on Ezra's nerves lately, "How many do you think she has?"

"No idea but from the sounds coming from her place and the number of feathers that are always floating around in the hallway, I'd guess dozens," Ezra shook his head, "or one gigantic one."

Nora laughed at the idea before turning back to Rowan, who was slowly stepping out into the hall, "Will you text me if it's anything important?" Nora asked.

"Of course, no problem. If not, I'll see you in the morning. Save me some coffee," he smiled with a wave and was gone.

Ezra clicked the locks back in place and turned to Nora, "Text you, huh? You guys are text buddies now?" He didn't look at her as he passed back to the couch.

"I mean, yeah. We're not completely shut out from the world. We're allowed to talk to people who work for The Firm," Nora looked him over when he plopped back down in front of the TV, "He's a nice guy, you know? You don't have to be such a bloody grump all the time."

"I know," he admitted, "I like him, too. I'd rather have him as my contact with Elijah than Gabriel, that's for sure," Ezra grumbled and grabbed the remote again. He flicked to the menu and scrolled the same shows and movies he always did.

"You have to try to get over lumping Gabriel in with the monsters like Jude," Nora said, pulling out a saucepan before Ezra became full-blown *hangry*, "He's been nothing but kind to us, and I know you know that. Who knows what would have happened to us – to your sister and her family – if he hadn't shown up for us."

"Yeah, I know you're right. I'm just going crazy in this place," he said and turned on the couch to watch Nora shuffling about in the kitchen, "Even if we can't leave this town, I want to be of use, you know? Not just a handyman for *this* place," he muttered with bitterness that told Nora he meant Jude's place.

Nora held up a pot and wooden spoon, "You could help with dinner, lazy ass."

Ezra smiled and stood up heavily from the couch to give her a hand. Even though her new apartment was much larger than the first-floor studio, the long island separating the counter and appliances against the wall made the kitchen area became tight when they worked together.

"You know what I mean, Nor. I want to be out there. I want to be proactive in all of

this," he reached up in the cupboard to grab a jar of pasta sauce, twisted off the lid, and dumped the contents in the pot Nora held, "Why can't I be out there with Rowan, and Melissa, and the crew? I want to help end all of this. I don't want to be the damsel in distress hidden away in the damn tower. I want to be on the ground, fighting the good fight with them."

Nora's expression fell as the faces of the crew they had trained with flashed in her memory, and she stopped on Angus. She had taken it to heart when he was killed in the raid on Jude's home. She was sure they were tipped off about the incoming attack because she had broken the rules and went to see her aunt. More than one person had assured her that a leak in The Firm was the cause and that she had nothing to do with the vampires lying in wait. That did not stop Angus' smiling face from clouding her memory with guilt and sorrow. She pushed the image away, not wanting to let herself fall into the depression that had been trying to take over her spirit for weeks.

"I don't know, Ez. I don't think it would be a good idea to try and join their BITN crew. Seeing as how keeping us away from vampires is their current assignment, having you out there with them would make it harder," Nora filled a pot with water and set it on the stove while Ezra pulled himself up to sit on the counter. Silas jumped up and curled himself up on his lap, purring happily.

"Yeah, I guess. There has to be something I could do, though. Maybe working with a crew that deals with a different kind of freak," he stopped when Nora pointed a wooden spoon at him in warning, "Sorry, supernaturals. Whatever."

They both turned quickly as the alarm on the counter started to beep. Silas jumped down at the irritating noise and made his way to the bedroom.

Sunset.

The alarm was set to go off every day five minutes before sunset. They moved from the kitchen and started their now regular routine of checking the locks on the windows, pulling down the shades that had been trimmed with thin silver chains, and triple checking the door. The phone rang on time, and Nora picked up to find Melissa's voice, ensuring they were settled in. She let them know that Zeke was on the night shift with them, as well as two recruits Nora had only met in passing. Melissa reassured her that she had checked on Jenny and Olivia in their apartment and asked her to call down when Ezra was ready to head down to his apartment for the night. After the sunset, it became the most dangerous time for the two, and they weren't allowed anywhere outside of their apartments if they were alone. Ezra was quite vocal that he deemed the escorts humiliating.

After working through their safety measures, they ate their dinner in silence on the couch and stared mindlessly at the television while sipping wine. There was no need to call down for an escort as Ezra fell asleep on her couch just as he had done most nights for the past few weeks. Nora pulled a blanket over him and went to bed with Silas on her heel. She always slept better when she could hear Ezra's quiet snore drifting into her bedroom. The soft sound let her know she was not alone. After re-checking her tall, silver-draped window, she crawled into bed and closed her eyes tight. The creaks and cracks she heard from the closed floor above her made her nerves twitch on edge. She repeated over and over to herself that they were nothing more than the sounds of a tired old building. The fantasy of leaving Aumbry Valley for good started as her paranoid mind twisted the creaking floor above into threateningly heavy footsteps. She eventually fell into one of her usual nightmares, running from a sky raining down red hot ash, her legs heavy and sinking into a ground made of thick blood. The sunrise could never come soon enough anymore.

CHAPTER TWO

THE HERMIT.
IX

When Nora came out of the bathroom the following day, twisting her wet hair up into a bun, Ezra was just waking up. He made a cranky show of stretching the kinks out of his back from sleeping on the couch as if it wasn't his choice to choose her sofa over his bed. Silas slinked past him and curled up on the pillow that had fallen to the floor. Nora's cat had taken to wandering out after she had fallen asleep to cuddle up with Ezra during the night. She was starting to wonder if the damn cat was beginning to prefer her new part-time roommate over her. Silas rubbed his head against Ezra's ankle, his lips and whiskers turned up in a contented smile as if he read her mind.

She fussed with the hair elastic, trying to rein in a few straggling locks before giving up and letting them fall. Being fussy about her looks was not something that Nora had ever spent much time on. Being clean and somewhat put together was enough. The girls in the elite boarding schools that Nora had been sent to had turned her off of the idea of self-obsession. In her opinion, the need for the newest, most expensive clothes and magazine-perfect makeup took up too much time, especially when the outcome was becoming a carbon copy of all the other girls who stressed in the mirror.

The fire-engine red that she preferred to dye her hair had faded away to a muddy pink stain on her light brown hair since she had stopped re-coloring it. The bright hue had been in honor of her beloved Cherry Bomb, the car Quinn had gifted her, and now that it had been destroyed and Quinn had become a stranger, even an enemy, to her, she had no desire to keep up the look. Ezra let out a loud yawn while he folded the blanket and tossed it on the back of the couch. He watched Nora tug at a faded lock of hair that dangled over her shoulder.

"The top of your head, that's your regular hair, right?" he asked, pointing to the roots of her hair.

"My regular hair?" Nora laughed, pushing the strand up into her bun, "My natural hair color, you mean?"

"Yeah, whatever it's called," he shrugged, "I like that color. It reminds me of gingerbread."

"My hair makes me look like a gingerbread man?" Nora laughed, filling the coffeemaker with water. There were worse things to look like, she decided.

"No, not like an actual gingerbread *man*, like gingerbread. The color of the cookie. Your hair is the color of the yummy cookies," Ezra said, popping his eyebrows up. He was nothing if not a foodie.

"Thank you, I think?" Nora offered with a crumpled scowl, even though she knew he meant it as a compliment. She was never good with compliments.

Ezra just shook his head with another shrug walking to the bathroom, "I'm just saying I like it. It's nice," he muttered as he closed the door.

Nora finished prepping the coffee and picked up her phone. Four missed texts from Gabriel. Nothing from Rowan. She frowned as she read the messages piled up from the nutty vampire.

Heeey Nora! How's the gilded cage treating you?
Is Ezra still making the e in his name stand for emo? Ha!

She smothered her laugh and looked at the closed bathroom door. Ezra whistled an unrecognizable song off-key as he went about his morning business.

I know you're probably sleeping. I'm stopping by tomorrow night for some window gossip. I have a couple of friends that want to meet you. Don't worry; King Elijah has granted me permission to HA!

The humor left her at the idea of new people being around her apartment. If they were friends of Gabriel's, they were most likely other vampires. The plus was that they wouldn't be able to enter the building; the worry was that Nora was having a much harder time trusting anyone over the past few months. Something that she was never very good at, to begin with. She pushed the anxiousness away and continued reading.

Things are finally happening! Which is good because I'm devastatingly bored with all of this.

I'll see you then. A bit after sunset. Tell Emozra I expect that big dazzling smile of his to welcome me.

Gabriel had started teasing Ezra endlessly since his cold shoulder to all vampires had emerged. Nora knew part of it was simply to hide the hurt of the sudden change in their relationship because real feelings weren't something the vampire dabbled in. Ezra had grown distant from him shortly after Gabriel had risked his own life to help save theirs, including Ezra's sister, sister-in-law, and niece. Even a flippant, devil-may-care vampire would feel the hurt of that reaction. The only hope she had for the two to be civil again was to be able to leave Dunhope Manor. Some space from the constant vigilance and reminders of Jude would help him to come around. The few distractions they had found for themselves were wearing thin, and Ezra quickly became a bump on a log with zero motivation except for his desire to join in the fight. Any fight.

The lack of information from anyone, including Gabriel and Elijah, made the time pass even slower and helped to build frustration and animosity towards the beings of Aumbry Valley. Being lowly humans that needed to be protected was something that Elijah seemed to have taken on more seriously than anyone on the Council, beings whom they had never met, and there was an appreciation for that. Even still, letting them in on paranormal business was not something Elijah was willing to stoop to. That left them with an unspoken release date and the worry about the many options of what they could be afraid of.

Nora glanced through the front door's peephole when she heard a knock and opened it to find Jenny standing in the hallway with Sarah. She was the waitress from Ezra's favorite restaurant in the valley, The Dirty Cantina, and a fellow witch in Jenny's coven. Yet another surprise to them.

Sarah had been around a lot since Ezra had been moved to the building. Nora had only met her briefly on her first night of being dropped into the supernatural world. She did not have an inkling of the waitress being anything more than a clueless townie living among the supernaturals in the Valley. Getting to know more about the coven members, she seemed to be Jenny's right-hand witch when it came to their dealings and had every reason to be around so much. Nora felt that the googly eyes that Sarah had permanently set on Ezra had a little more to do with it. She knew they had been on a few dates when he first arrived in town. He insisted it was nothing and blushed whenever Nora or Jenny brought it up.

When Ezra appeared from the bathroom, Sarah held up a tote bag that was filled to the brim with Styrofoam takeout containers.

"I thought I'd find you here," she chirped to him, with a quick glance to Nora, "I figured your fridge was due for a refill."

Ezra moved quickly to the bag and deeply inhaled the aroma of Mexican food that the bag held, "You are too good to me, Sarah! Is there…"

Sarah interrupted the question, "The avocado salsa is in the top container. Extra hot, just like you like," she gave him a wide toothy smile and handed him the bag. She smoothed the curls that fell over her shoulder, watching him dig through the offerings.

"Aw, yeah! You're the best! If it's witchcraft that makes this taste this good, you're the best witch in the world! " Ezra exclaimed and gave her a light punch on her arm, taking the bag to the counter.

"Nope, just the owner's recipes. They're not spells, as far as I know," she giggled.

Silas sidled up to him, circling his leg and sniffing up at the food before jumping on the counter. Ezra pulled a small piece of chicken from one of the containers to give to the begging cat. Nora shook her head in disapproval. Maybe the cat didn't prefer Ezra over Nora; it was Ezra's taste in food. Silas gave a narrow-eyed stare to Sarah and rubbed his cheek against the bag.

"Yeah, well. It's no problem," Sarah said before giving the group a tight grin, "Oh! Do you still have that book we were talking about? The one about that guy who jumped from the plane. I was hoping to borrow it."

"The Cooper book! Of course, I do. It's not like I could go anywhere with it," Ezra said with a snort. He grabbed a mug and filled it with the freshly brewed coffee, offering an empty mug to Sarah, who shook her head no, "All right, come on down, and I'll find it for you. It's a good read."

He grabbed the saltshaker and sprinkled a dash into the coffee, just as Nora took it. He had been grossed out the first time he saw her do it, and it took weeks to convince him to try it. Now he couldn't have it without it. Sarah and Jenny's noses turned up in revolt. They were not fans.

"Bring back that mug this time, please! I'm guessing your sink is filled with all of my dirty mugs," Nora called out as they headed out and down the stairs. Ezra raised the mug back at her in acknowledgment.

Jenny watched them leave before picking up the extra cup that Ezra had left out, "That girl can not get over him. I mean, it was two dates. If you ask me, it was a date and a half, really."

Nora smiled when Jenny swung open the fridge to grab the milk. She enjoyed her friend's ease in her apartment. After the few months that Nora was pinching pennies and continuously late on her rent, it was nice to have full cupboards to share with Jenny, even if it was being bankrolled by a group of supernatural beings and not from her own hard work.

"I think it's cute. I guess it's probably hard to know when you're ready to date after going through what he did," Nora thought of Ezra's heartbreaking words when he described the night that Jude had destroyed his family, "I don't think Ezra even notices women anymore, thanks to all of this, though. He's so frustrated," Nora said quietly.

"Maybe if he did notice them, he wouldn't be so frustrated," Jenny exclaimed with a cocked brow and a laugh.

"Yeah, maybe," Nora smiled half-heartedly, "It's not like he can hit the town looking for someone. The options are pretty limited within this building. No wonder he's so frustrated."

"Speaking of frustrated, how's Rowan doing? You getting anywhere with that?"

Nora rolled her eyes, "He's good. Should be here any minute," she replied coyly.

"He's *good,* is he?" Jenny leaned her elbows on the counter, her mug clutched in both hands.

"Not like that, Jenny. Come on," Nora laughed and turned back to the door when there was another knock, "And how would I get a chance to know anyways? This place has been Grand Central Station lately."

She looked through the peephole to find Rowan standing on the other side of the door. Heat raced over her cheeks, and she turned back to Jenny to raise a shush finger to her lips. Even though nothing between the two had happened beyond flirting, a flutter in her stomach always stirred when he was around. Dunhope Manor had started to become one of the nonsense reality shows that she and Ezra had become addicted to. Hormones, tantrums, and redecorating. The constant threat of the undead and various supernatural characters seemed to be the only difference between the shows and their current reality.

"Hey. How was your night?" Rowan questioned, giving Jenny a friendly nod.

"Quiet, like usual," Nora reported. As she started to close the door, Elijah brushed past into the apartment; a grin spread across his face.

"Come on in, I guess," Nora muttered to the new visitor. She retrieved the cream from the fridge when Rowan poured his coffee. He didn't know that Nora kept it on hand solely for him.

"Nora, my dear, I come bearing wonderful news," he said, clasping his hands with excitement. Nora's heart rate picked up with anticipation of whatever he could be about to share, as it did whenever he would have the most minor update. Whatever it was, it was good news to Elijah. He turned to see Jenny and Rowan, "Oh! Hello, Ms. Duran! Mr. Andries. I'm glad you're here to receive the wonderful news. We have gotten word that Quinn has been located and will soon be brought before the Council!"

"So, she's...." Nora's breath caught, and she steadied herself against the kitchen island.

"She is indeed alive, yes. Well, still *undead* as it is," Elijah said, smiling when a relieved gasp escaped from Nora, "She should be in custody and transported within the day."

The news she had been waiting for did not bring her expected relief. Quinn was still on the top side of the soil and now surrounded by agents of The Firm. Nora should have felt free and excited. The release from Dunhope Manor had to be imminent with Quinn's threat eliminated. Instead, she could not shake the feeling that there was another shoe to drop. After months of being locked down, it seemed too simple to be able to walk out of the building and straight out of town. Since the vamp crazies who were in her aunt's pseudo-cult had used the destruction of her car as a threat, she would now need transportation. Ezra still had his Jeep, even though he had not been allowed access to it since they had been cloistered away. She wondered if he would give her a ride. If they were able to leave. If they were allowed to hit the road and leave everything behind them. Her mind spun with possibilities, and she wished Ezra would return to hear the news. Her knees wobbled with the avalanche of questions that took over her thoughts, and she perched on a kitchen stool.

"What's going to happen? With Quinn?" Nora queried, her voice low. Her freedom could mean her aunt's demise. Quinn's bright smile, before it had been framed with fangs, shone in her memories.

"That will be up to the Council. They will determine her responsibility, along with her current threat level, and then decide what her future will be," Elijah stopped when worry crossed Nora's tight expression, "I can tell you that she will most likely be interrogated at length and then be moved to the Council's Bastille."

"The what? What's that?" Nora asked, not liking the sounds of it.

"It is a jail of sorts that is set up to accommodate the many sorts of beings that they oversee," he placed a hand gently on Nora's shoulder, "It's not as bad as you can imagine, and it is a much more favorable outcome than a final death. I am told she surrendered peacefully and is willing to provide important information to the council. The first intelligent decision she has made may have spared her life."

Jenny put a hand on Nora's other slumped shoulder, "What does all of this mean for Nora and Ezra? I guess for all of us? How close are we to moving on from this mess?" Her calm demeanor seemed an ill fit for such important news. Nora wondered what all Jenny had been through as a witch living in a town of vampires, demons, fae, and god knows who else. The capture of a vindictive vampire that had her sights set on her tenant was most likely *not* the most terrifying moment in her life. The unimaginable possibilities made Nora both eager to leave the valley and sad to leave her friend behind.

"It is too soon to tell. However, we are certainly coming to a welcome conclusion. We shall keep things as they are for now until we have a decision from the Council and the final word has been spoken. I suppose it is not too soon to start thinking of plans for the future, Nora. If you will stay with us or move on to greener pastures. I believe I speak for all of us when I say I hope you choose to stay. I do still believe you to be a good fit with us. You have proven yourself quite the tough little mortal. One I would prefer to have on my side of any altercations that may come."

Nora didn't know where to start processing her options and could only slightly lift the corners of her lips. Staying on would mean financial stability and the bizarre family unit that she had begun to create. It also meant monsters, danger, and the insanity of a supernatural world she knew she did not belong in.

Elijah interrupted her spinning thoughts, "Is there anything else you need in the meantime?"

Nora shook her head, knowing that all she wanted was information she would still have to wait patiently for, "Have you told Ezra?"

"I have not. I assumed he would be here," Elijah replied, looking around the room as if he would pop up from behind furniture. He gave Rowan a quizzical look when he sputtered a laugh at what he had said.

"He's down in his apartment," Nora advised, "with Sarah."

"Oh, right then. Shall I tell him the news, or would you prefer to do the honors?" Elijah asked, glowing with the excitement of the newest revelation.

"It would probably be better if you told him. He'll probably have questions," Nora said, knowing he would. Not that he could pull much else out of the suitably stiff demon.

Elijah gave a quick nod to them and was out the door without another word as was his way. He was constantly processing the next task to deal with before he was finished with his current one. With how much he was always dealing with, she had told the busy demon repeatedly that a text or phone call was much quicker than coming all the way over for a two-minute conversation. Elijah insisted that telephones were for gossip or the long-distance business of mortals. He preferred to set eyes on her when he had news. She noticed that he sneered when he was forced to answer his phone. Nora was getting used to his quirky ways and had started to find them endearing.

As he passed out into the hallway, Norman, the shut-in from next door, watched him pass from his open door. They shared nothing more than a curt bob of their heads. Norman's investigative eyes peered into Nora's apartment. She was glad he was slowly getting used to having a neighbor and was starting to warm up to the idea of people passing by his door. Even if they were demons, witches, and mortals who did the bidding of the supernatural underworld. Nora was sure that the less Norman knew, the better. They did not have what you would call visits by any means, but he did not hide behind his door as much and would occasionally say hello. He was keener to interact when Olivia was with them, his own childlike spirit seeming kindled with the three-year-old. They had struck up a sweet friendship that helped Norman come out of his shell just a sliver, and Jenny was thankful for the calming effect he seemed to have on the energetic toddler. Today appeared to be a brave day for him when he smiled at the trio next door.

"Hey Norman, how're you doing today?" Jenny asked, moving towards the door.

"I'm good, I'm good," he said quietly, looking from her to the now empty staircase, "Everything okay with you guys today?"

"All good with us, Norman. Did you want to come over and say hello to Nora and our friend Rowan?" Jenny smiled gently.

Norman moved a step back into the safe space behind him, his eyes flickering between Jenny, Nora, and Rowan, "No...no, thank you. There is an issue with the window in my sitting room that I'd like you to have someone look at. It sticks." Norman and Gail were more than happy to have their apartments brought back to life with Ezra's handy work ever since he had taken up residency.

"I'll ask Ezra to take a look when he has time, all right?" Jenny chuckled when he nodded quickly and closed the door between them. That was enough socializing for him for the day.

"He was almost chatty that time," Rowan laughed.

"A virtual social butterfly, that one," Jenny said with a smile at the tightly closed door, "Anyways, I should get going, too. Olivia is only on her playdate for another hour, and I have a ton of stuff to get done," Jenny rinsed her mug out and set it in the sink.

"Do you think it's safe out there for her to be having playdates?" Nora worried aloud.

"As safe as it always was, girl. The craziness didn't arrive with you, and it's not going to leave with you," Jenny sighed and gave a quick hug before heading out for her day.

Rowan cleared his throat, "She's right, you know?" This town has always been and will always be chaos. But that's part of its charm."

"I'm not such a fan of chaos. Especially the type that can kill you," she jeered.

"There are times that chaos chooses you, and there's nothing you can do but ride the wave until you hit the shore. It's worth the struggle when you have no other choice," Rowan offered.

"I prefer to stay out of the water completely," Nora assured him.

"Gotta get wet sometimes, Nora," Rowan mused, finishing the last of his coffee and heading for the door, "I'll be downstairs if you need anything. I'll let you know if we hear anything else."

"Thanks, Rowan," Nora murmured, hiding the fresh blush on her cheeks as she shut the door behind him and fashioned the locks closed.

The apartment was empty again and far too quiet. She put the containers of food that Ezra had left out on the counter into the fridge and looked around the room. Her apartment itself had become waves of chaos and calm. At that moment, she realized she no longer enjoyed the tranquility of loneliness that used to be her normal. She stared out the window and down to the street. A few cars passed by. People were going about their day without any idea of what existed around them. Just as Nora once did.

She shut the curtain to block out the world. Even if she could leave, she would never be the same. If she could convince Gabriel to wipe her mind, she would be just like the helpless people she watched from her window. If he didn't, she would never truly leave Aumbry Valley in her past.

Deciding first things first, she would wait to find out what would happen to Quinn. Then she would be able to step foot outside of Dunhope Manor. After that, she would figure out the rest. Ride the wave, as Rowan had said. Her face heated again, remembering his words.

Gotta get wet, sometimes, Nora.

CHAPTER THREE

XVI
THE TOWER.

Nora kept her mind busy for most of the day by tidying her apartment and then tidying it again. She had been attempting to lose herself in trying her hand at painting over the last couple of months, something that she had found as an escape as a child. The skyscape she had been working on stared back at her before she gave up in frustration, unable to bring her mind to a happy place to recreate the distant memory on canvas. The flow of visitors that she had become used to had dried up for the day, and each of her footsteps on the hard wooden floors echoed against the walls. Silas soon grew weary of her pacing and retired to the bedroom for his afternoon nap after Nora had straightened the bedspread for the third time.

Sending a text to Ezra, she wondered if Sarah was still with him and hoped she wasn't being a bother. When no response was received, she assumed he was pre-occupied and did not want to intrude by going down for a visit.

She was alone with her thoughts. With her worries. She pulled out the broom again.

She bound towards the door when Jenny popped in again after lunch, this time with Olivia, to ask if any word on Quinn had arrived. Nora shook her head no, not wanting to get too deep into her worry in front of Olivia. The little girl could always make Nora smile, and the visit was more than a welcome distraction.

"Hey Norma, guess what?" the little girl asked. Nora loved how she always mispronounced her name.

"What?" Nora asked, her eyes wide with exaggerated excitement.

"In two weeks, I'm gonna be this many," she squealed, holding up four fingers, "and I want to have a party!"

"Holy moly! You're already going to be four! You're growing up so fast!" Nora exclaimed and handed her a juice box. Olivia turned it away from Jenny when she tried to help her with the straw. She was as stubborn as her mother and gave her a toothless grin when she succeeded in piercing the box, taking a celebratory gulp from the small bendy straw.

"Yep, and I want you to come!" she crowed.

Silas strolled out to see what all of the commotion was and turned tail back into the bedroom when he saw Olivia bouncing around the apartment.

"Well, I wouldn't miss it for the world. Thank you for inviting me," Nora said, giving the little girl's frizzy brown ponytail a playful tug.

"I want you to come, and mommy, and Ezra, and the dancing girl, and we're going to have chocolate cupcakes!" she shouted and ran off to chase a grumpy Silas into the bedroom.

"The dancing girl?" Nora asked Jenny with a laugh, "Who is that?"

"Yeah, apparently it's her new *friend*," Jenny said with air quotes, "The age of invisible friends has started."

Nora gave an uncomfortable chuckle, "In a town like this, how can you be sure she's imaginary?" Especially in such a creaky old building that looked straight out of a ghost story. She wasn't sure how she would handle finding out that, along with not being allowed to leave there, it was haunted by the spirits of creepy little children.

"Because this place is spellbound tight, Nora. Don't worry. No one supernatural is getting in or out. Besides, I was the same way when I was her age," Jenny said reassuringly for her spooked friend.

"What about ghosts? Could she have ghost friends?" Nora asked, feeling ridiculous and uncomfortable all in the same breath.

"It's not ghosts, Nora. Seriously. Don't worry. She just started going on about this friend for the past week or so. I doubt the ghost of a little girl randomly found her way here to befriend my daughter," Jenny stated matter-of-factly with a hand on her nervous friend's shoulder.

Ghosts suddenly appearing did not seem impossible with all that Nora had experienced so far. What was normal to Jenny was undoubtedly not commonplace to her. It seemed best to follow the witch's lead for what should be a worry and what should not. After years of living in a town filled with things Nora believed to be fiction, Jenny was far more knowledgeable about what was real and what was not. Nora set aside her jumble of thoughts to watch the little girl whizz by after the unimpressed cat and laughed.

"So, has there been anything more from Elijah today?" Jenny asked, changing the subject.

Nora frowned and shook her head, "Nothing yet."

"No news is good news, I guess," Jenny offered with a tight smile.

They made light, distracting conversation until Olivia announced she was bored and headed for the door. Nora promised to call if there was any news and went back to pacing when they had departed back down to the main floor.

When there was still no word from Ezra, the anxiety bubbled up from her stomach and started to build in her chest. It was strange to her how uncomfortable she had become being alone in the past few months. Fear of the unknown aside, she now enjoyed the company. She turned up the television to drown out the creaks of the building and picked up her phone to call Rowan. Her lips curled into a put-off frown when he quickly got her off the phone, saying they had nothing new to pass on, but he was headed to the office to meet with his higher-ups. He promised to call her later, but her anxiety wound tighter in her stomach.

Eventually, Nora heard Ezra knocking at Norman's door, saying he was there to take to a look at the window, and relief started to ease the knot building in her shoulders. She ignored the fact that she looked at her watch to add up the hours he had spent in his apartment with Sarah. If she was even there. She ignored that thought, as well, and told herself that she was just not very good at being alone anymore.

He knocked on her door after about twenty minutes, just under an hour before the sunset warning alarm would sound on her counter, and she opened it to him with a welcoming smile.

"Hey. How are you holding up?" he asked, sitting at the counter while Nora pulled frozen burgers from the fridge, "I haven't heard a thing from anyone all day. Did Elijah call you?"

"Nope. I'm mostly trying not to think about what's going on out there," Nora grumbled.

"How long could it possibly take to grab one little crazy vampire?" Ezra wondered aloud, and his shoulders sank a bit when he saw Nora's level stare, "You know what I mean. I'm starting to think these supes aren't all that skilled at what they do. How they've survived and stayed in secret all this time without being able to handle this one little problem is incredible."

"We don't know *what* they're doing or who they're coming up against, Ez. We're not the humans they give any info to; the ones they do are just as tight-lipped."

"That's exactly what I mean! We're just supposed to sit here and take their word that they're out there doing whatever the hell they're doing? How do we know that they don't already have Quinn or that she isn't even the threat that they say she is?" Ezra stood to pace the room, his hands wildly waving with each new question, "We're just supposed to take their word because, why? They're superior beings? They used us to get to Jude, they're using people to do their bidding in the crews, and who's to say they aren't using us for something else now?"

The flood of questions startled an awareness within her. She had always prided herself as a seeker of answers. So much so that she had to force herself to bite her tongue in situations where her inquisitions had become bothersome and intrusive. Everything that Ezra was positing was what she would have been obsessing over. With the incredible amount of new information that had been dumped on her with the new knowledge of the supernatural world and her place within it, she had gone numb to react. She found herself taking the word of those that seemed at home in the crazy world that was holding her in place. They were keeping her safe and could easily navigate the secrets of Aumbry Valley. It was easy to let them take the wheel, no questions asked. There was a difference between trusting Jenny, a friend, and blindly following what the bureau and The Firm as a whole would even allow her to know. The realization came in a blink of an eye, and she steadied herself with her palms pressed to the counter. She had lost the parts of herself that she valued when she tried to find herself in a world where she felt she did not belong. Ezra was pushing to be proactive. He wanted to be in control of his life. Nora had begun to use the loss of power as an excuse to hide from the bizarre reality she found herself in. She needed to stop thinking that waiting was the only thing she could do.

"What would they possibly gain from keeping us in Dunhope Manor, of all places?" Nora wondered aloud.

Ezra perched on the stool again, his hands tapping in front of him as he thought, "I really don't know. We could still be bait, I guess. They could still be planning to punish us for taking the lives of vamps. I don't know. They didn't seem to care that I took out Harper at Mystique, and she was trying to kill you," his face tightened as he considered other reasons, "Maybe they're Hansel and Gretel'ing us. You know, fattening us up to make us a meal?" he said and looked to Nora. The idea had them both out of the anxious what-ifs moment and cracking a laugh.

"So, they're going to feed us to Jenny? The big bad witch?" Nora added with a snort.

"Yeah, so probably not that," Ezra conceded, "but you have to admit, it's hard not to let your mind roam when they don't tell us anything."

"Yeah, I see your point," Nora mumbled, telling herself that she would not be as keen to go with the flow any longer. Hopefully, at any moment, they would get word that the worst was over, and they could move forward with their lives. Whatever that would be, "I can't stand the waiting. That's the worst part of not knowing. Sitting around trying not to think about how much I need to know the little crumb of information they'll give us."

Ezra shifted on the stool, "So Rowan hasn't been keeping you in the loop today?"

"Nothing. Nada," Nora sighed and tossed a bag of hamburger buns on the counter, "How was your day? I texted you, but I figured you were still having a visit when you didn't respond," Nora teased.

"I didn't see you texted," Ezra said, patting his pockets, "Wait, Where's my phone?" He patted his pockets again and looked at his watch. Thirty-seven minutes until they had to have escorts in the building. He was out the door in a flash. When he didn't return after a few minutes, Nora opened the door and peered out, listening for any sound of him. Looking to the floor, she watched a shadow appear at Norman's door, the light disappearing behind his peephole. She gave a wave she knew he would see, stepped back inside, and clicked her door closed. Nora wondered how he would react if he knew the scope of the insanity that was happening all around him and under his own roof. If what he knew of the world frightened him, she was sure that the reality would have him boarding up his windows and doors for good.

She twisted the locks and busied herself with preparing dinner. It was almost twenty minutes before he returned, with a look of frustration scrunching his face.

"What's up?" Nora asked, flipping the burger patties in the pan.

"I can't find my phone anywhere down there," he muttered, flipping up her couch cushions on the hunt for his cell. He stood straight up, hands on his hips, eyes scanning the apartment when he failed to find it.

"It has to be here somewhere or down there. It's not like you could have dropped it on the sidewalk," Nora concluded with a frown.

"Obviously, but I have no idea where it is."

Nora shrugged and set about finishing dinner. When the alarm rang out to warn of the soon-to-be setting sun, they went about their routine before sitting down for burgers and salad. Ezra poked at the lettuce before starting on the vegetables with a grumble. It was hard to complain about what was served when he had every meal prepared for him. Nora snickered at the grown man pouting over having to eat his veggies.

After they finished, she found herself frowning when Zeke Terrell called up to check in, not Rowan. Zeke was a sweet hulk of a man, and she felt terrible for being curt with him, but there had been no word from Rowan since he said he was headed to a meeting with his bosses. There was certainly no obligation for him to let her in on any of what he was told; it was his job, after all. She thought their friendship had started to evolve to a place where he would trust her with a little more of what was being kept from her. It worried her that what he discovered was worse than she could imagine. Rubbing her temples, she pushed away the avalanche of possibilities that swallowed her mind. Her nerves were getting the best of her without a single word from Elijah. They had gotten used to not being kept in the loop, but this was different. This felt like they were almost at the finish line of the most terrifying months of her life, and it was a rotten time for the minutes to start feeling like hours.

They had just loaded the last of the dishes in the dishwasher when they jumped at the sound of Gabriel's distinctive three-two-three knock on the living room window. It had taken some time for them to become comfortable with the vampire casually leaning on the windowsill of the third-floor apartment while his velvet-slippered feet hovered high above the sidewalk. The spells on the building had made him get creative with how he could visit, and he had found this to be the next best thing. Nora was always happy to see the jovial vamp arrive to cheer her up, even if Ezra wasn't.

When they opened the curtain, they were surprised to find two strangers floating alongside Gabriel, with their fanged smiles directed at them. Nora had forgotten that he mentioned visitors in his text. The two men were flanking Gabriel in the air like a *ying and yang*: one with piercing blue eyes and buttery blonde hair, the other with hair as dark as ink and deep-set mocha eyes.

"Nora! My gorgeous blood bag, how are you holding up?" Gabriel said, holding up a dusty bottle of wine, "I snagged this for you from...ah, let's call him a *friend* for Ezra's sake."

Nora knew that was code for someone that had been Gabriel's latest meal. Nora smothered her grin even as she found it foul. The details of the life of a vampire were usually more interesting to Nora than to the vamp-hating Ezra. Finding out that one of the jobs assigned to the few humans in the know of the supernatural underbelly of the valley was to be a feeder, someone who donated blood right from the source, was one fact that grossed her out more than intrigued her. Gabriel had taken to raiding wine cellars and pantries of the wealthier meals in an attempt to rustle up gifts to cheer her up. Nora had scolded him for stealing from people who were already opening their veins to him before he assured her that he had no qualms about taking whatever he wanted. The feeders were granted benefits from their inclusion in the paranormal world that outweighed a thing or two he would nick after getting his fill.

Ezra glared over her shoulder at the bottle and then at each of the vampires. Nora rolled her eyes when he scoffed and stomped over to the couch. She knew he would have no issue sampling a glass once the visitors had left.

"Hi there, Ezra. I see you're as chipper as always," Gabriel snarked, setting the wine on the windowsill for Nora to take. She paused, looking at the strangers, unsure if it would be safe to let her hand cross the threshold, and Gabriel put his hands on their arms, "It's okay. These are the good guys, Nora. Go ahead," he assured, nodding at the bottle.

She braved her hand on the bottle and had to launch her other one out when she almost toppled it to the sidewalk below, "Oh shit!"

Gabriel put a hand to his chest when she safely placed it on the table beside her, "Someone doesn't have much fae juju left in them. That's a nine-hundred-dollar bottle of grapes there, girl! Be careful!"

"What? Nine hundred dollars? Holy crap!" Her speed and reflexes were quickly slowing as the serum started to fade and leave her system. Ezra had even begun to be a little more clumsy, just as he said he had been before going through the Ascension. Nora looked over the bottle, wiping the dust from the label, and held it up to Ezra, who was trying to seem disinterested. She sat it down on the side table and turned back to her visitors with a frustrated sigh, "So, tell me you have news."

"Sorry, no. Other than *she's* on her way back here," Gabriel offered, his eyes scanning the street below, "They'll deal with the bitch soon enough."

"Gabriel!" Nora scolded. She ignored Ezra's snort of amusement that he let slip as he pretended to flick through the options on the television, his head turned slightly to the side to avoid missing a shared word.

"What? Like she's your favorite person anymore?" Gabriel barked, "Anyways, I want you to meet Jimmy and Yosef, or *Yimmy* as I like to call them."

Nora smothered a laugh when Gabriel exclaimed it to sound more like yummy, with a saucy flick of his eyebrow, "Hi, nice to meet you," she greeted them and looked to Gabriel for an explanation of why they were there. It had been enough of a security risk to have him visit her as if she were Rapunzel in the tower; she was sure the crew wouldn't be happy that he was now bringing along random strangers.

"Yimmy here is going to help make sure that crazy aunt of yours never sees the light of the moon again," Gabriel explained, proudly smiling, "Jimmy was one of the team members that tracked her down. Yosef was one of the dummies that fell for Jude's preaching and luckily wised up in time to get out."

Ezra stood quickly from the couch and glared at the two before stomping for the door, "I'm out of here, Nora."

"Ez, don't be like that," Nora pleaded, "They're here to help."

"Help? Yeah, sure. Vampires are a great help. Especially ones that are friends with Jude," he muttered bitterly and started to unlock the door.

"He just said he's not, Ezra. Not anymore, at least," Nora pleaded as he opened the door, "If you want to leave, at least call down for an escort."

"I don't need a fucking escort. For god's sake, I'm a grown-ass man," he shouted, stepping out the doorway into the dark hallway, "If Norman and Gail can come and go as they please, so can I. Even Olivia has more freedom in this goddamn building."

The door was slammed before Nora could make it across the room. She paused, hand on the knob, worried about what Ezra may do. At least the slam of his door below let her know that he had been smart enough to stay in the building. She secured the locks again, double-checking them as she always did, and returned to her window's floating guests.

"Let Emozra sulk, Nora. He'll come around once he can get his *grown-ass* outside again," Gabriel consoled, "More wine for you, anyways," he winked.

Nora was hoping that would be the case and that it would happen sooner rather than later. The news of her capture that morning felt like it had been delivered days ago.

"So, you both know Quinn? Or *knew* her?" she asked, trying to picture her aunt chumming around with vampires. She had always had out there taste in friends, so it wasn't that surprising with all she had been learning about Quinn's path to Jude and Aumbry Valley. Vampire friends didn't seem a stretch for a woman who kept company with shamans, new-age gurus, and even a woman who self-identified as a messenger for the sun. She wasn't a lady who lunched like her mother.

"I was dumb enough to fall for Jude's lies before he even knew her, but I met her a few times before I wised up and got the hell out of there," the dark-haired man named Yosef said with remorse dripping from his words, "I can't believe how many of us almost...," he stopped to shake his head, looking towards the twinkling lights of the houses that dotted the lush hills behind them where Jude had resided, "I can't even think about how wrong things could have gone. How much *more* wrong than they did."

"Luckily, most of them smartened up when Jude was done. I think seeing a small little human take him out took some of the shine from his god-like status," Jimmy said with a laugh. Nora didn't reciprocate. Jude was a monster and would have taken many more lives if he hadn't been stopped. Even so, that didn't make her feel any better that her hand had stopped him. The nightmares she had every night made sure to remind her how much it had impacted her and that it was a part of who she would be for the rest of her life. She was someone who now knew that she was capable of taking a life, even if it was the life of someone undead.

"There doesn't seem to be anyone that will admit to supporting Quinn anymore. The insanity of what they were trying to accomplish was pretty clear when they were able to step back and see the big picture. If the maker's body had been destroyed, man," Yosef said and shook his head at the thought, "You don't fuck with the fae, that's for sure."

Before anyone could reply, a burst of wind pushed through the window, causing her to lose her balance, and she toppled back to the ground, the bottle of wine shattering beside her.

"Shut that window and lock it, now!" a voice roared from outside.

Nora pulled herself to her feet to find that the gust had resulted from the arrival of a half dozen more vampires who had joined the group in the air outside the window.

"What the hell is going on?" Gabriel demanded with surprise.

Nora froze when she heard heavy footfalls pounding up the stairs and voices shouting on the other side of her door as keys twisted in the locks. She stood barefoot in the burgundy puddle of shattered glass and wine when Melissa stormed into the room and moved quickly for her with another four guards.

"Nora, get away from the window. She's loose. Quinn broke free of the convoy."

CHAPTER FOUR

XVIII
THE MOON.

"Where is Ezra?" Melissa demanded, closing the locks on the window and pulling the blind down quickly, "What the hell were you thinking having this open?"

Nora opened and closed her mouth, unable to answer. They had been loose with the tight security whenever Gabriel had visited and had never made a fuss. It had never felt like a risk with him there, especially now with the expectation that Quinn was to be in custody at any moment. Melissa's face was tense, her eyes constantly scanning the room. Her usual friendly smile and playful giggle were nowhere to be found when she grabbed Nora's wrist and pulled her to her feet and away from the window. Nora's pulse pounded in her ears with the sudden fear that washed over her.

Zeke and Rowan thundered into the room with Ezra, who was unimpressed with being dragged by his arm up the stairs. He pulled away and tugged his sleeves down when they set him on the couch beside a speechless Nora. They sat and watched the frenzied movements of the crew, checking the windows and shouting into cell phones. Zeke started to close the door but stopped and used his mountainous body as a blockade when Jenny's voice called out as she bound up the stairs.

"What is going on?" she shouted over the chaos as she joined the group. Nora's apartment started to feel claustrophobic quickly.

"Jenny, get Olivia and get back up here as fast as you can," Melissa said, her professional calm seeping back in, "We need everyone together for now."

"What about Gail and Norman?" she asked, raising her hand to knock on his door. Zeke grabbed her wrist before she could.

"They're not part of our orders. Get Olivia and get your butt back here. Please, Jenny. Go," Melissa implored, her voice softening.

Nora was not happy about the other two residents being left out of the security they were being provided. With all of the commotion, there was no way that Norman didn't hear the raised voices. She hoped that would have been enough for him to want to avoid the hallway and anyone in it, keeping him a little bit safer inside his own walls.

"Why are you all freaking out about one tiny little vampire? We were already on lockdown before she was caught. What's the big deal now? What is really going on?" Ezra bellowed, banging his palm on the back of the couch, demanding they answer him.

Nora looked from him to the gathered group when her eyes started to feel heavy, her eyelids lazily blinking from their newly heavy weight, and her body became weightless in her seat. The smell of sugar cookies enveloped the room and swirled around her like a warm, soothing blanket fresh from the dryer. A dopey smile pulled at her lips when three of the Glamor Guards, the ridiculously gorgeous fae security for The Firm, swept into the apartment. Two Amazonian blond women and a caramel-headed beast of a man with a trim beard to match took up more space than their bodies should. They zeroed in on Nora.

"Miss. Goodman, has Quinn Goodman been in contact with you in any form?" the first of the golden-locked fairy asked. Her voice was light and hypnotic, the polar opposite of the angry, fire-lit eyes she had locked on hers.

"Nope," Nora said with a giggle. She reached out and booped the woman on the nose. The fairy swatted her hand away, keeping her eyes in an unblinking stare.

The second woman stepped forward to speak, "Do you have any idea what her plans might be? Miss. Goodman, tell us everything you know."

Nora had sunk deep into the comfort of the fae's effect. Whether the shock of the intrusion, the news that Quinn had broken free, or if they were using a much stronger effort on her, the room became hazy, warm, and tucking her into a comfortable slumber. She forced her eyes open and drifted her attention around the room to the crew floating about, appearing to move in slow motion while securing the space. Nora wondered why they were moving so slowly and why she couldn't hear them. A buzz in her ears, low and steady, started to build and relax her mind. Her sightline dragged to the kitchen, and she found Ezra sitting on the stool. She didn't remember him moving from the couch beside her. She giggled and looked from the empty cushion and back to him. He stared back with a look of concern for her. Nora liked the way the light of the room cast shadows on his face. She wondered what he would look like in candlelight. She let out a slow, secretive chuckle at what she pictured doing with him in the candlelight.

"Nora, Nora. You're so naughty," she murmured, putting her tired head down on the back of the couch. Her eyes narrowed when she couldn't recall what she had just been thinking. The effect of the three agitated fae was starting to make her nauseous.

The male stepped forward and snapped in her face to get her attention. She had to take a minute to focus on him.

Nora sluggishly raised her eyebrow when her eyes could take him in, "Yowza. How are you doing? You're a warm little gingersnap, aren't you?" she gave a half smile when she unsuccessfully tried to snap her fingers. A rumble of voices vibrated across the room, and the upset building in her stomach grew when she tried to decipher what was being said. She groaned and set her head down again. The comfortable room around her turned on her and started to spin.

"Miss. Goodman. What are Quinn Goodman's plans?" he repeated.

"No idea. Probably something bad," Nora laughed, tracing the man's beard with a lazy finger. She swallowed the rush of saliva that gave warning of her stomach's eruption and frowned.

A voice broke through the haze, and the three fae stepped away from her, "All right, that's enough, please. You're overdoing it," Elijah's prim voice demanded, "She has very little serum left in her bloodstream. You will turn her mind to pudding if you keep at it."

The three fae looked to Elijah with frustration before stepping back from Nora. The room started to lose the bubbly sparkle. The warm, cozy cocoon gave way to the deep heat radiating from Elijah. The demon had an air about him that no one in the room, even the omni-powerful fae, wanted to press against.

"Elijah, what's going on? Tell us the truth," Ezra demanded, filling a glass of water for Nora. She was thankful when he handed it to her, and she shook away more of the parting haze before gulping it to refresh her dry mouth. Holding what was left in the cool glass against the throbbing in her head, she groaned. The hangover from a super-fae effect was much worse than just the usual fatigue. It felt more like an attack than a simple influence of energy. She struggled to regain focus and process what was happening around her. She looked from window to window, each with a member of the BITN security crew in front, and then to the shattered wine that was now staining the floor.

"Ezra, please. We must..." Elijah stiffened and seemed to grow several inches in height when Ezra moved forward to interrupt him. Whatever he saw in the demon's eyes froze him in place. For a brief moment, Elijah pressed a palm to his own head, regaining his staunch composure, "I am sorry. It is just…" he sighed, loosening his tie less than an inch, and pulled in a breath that seemed to reach all the way down to his feet, before releasing it in a quick burst, "All right. All right. You are right. You do need to know," he smoothed a lock of his salt and pepper hair that had escaped his thick pomade, "Quinn was not as complacent as we had thought. The depth of her reach within our bureau is far more dangerous than we could have ever imagined," he stole a shared glace with the caramel-haired fairy whose bearded jaw twitched with tension, "Quinn had the chamber breached, by whom we are not yet sure, and she has secured the blood of the Maker," Elijah spoke flatly, his face drawn with defeat.

"What does that mean? What chamber?" Ezra asked, fear and frustration setting his feet to pacing, "The maker? The original vamp that you guys were going to kill?" he asked the tall fairy that stood impossibly still beside him. She ignored him and kept her attention on Elijah.

"Yes. He was being kept within a crypt in the council's aumbry, a chamber that was thought to be impossible to enter unless you had the authority to do so. It was also, unfortunately, believed that Jude was a lone madman. All of our intel pointed to this. Everything pointed to that fact," Elijah said through angry, gritted teeth. The usual aristocratic calm that he exuded was having difficulty staying in place, "Quinn has shown us who the true threat is. The chamber of the aumbry that holds the body of the one true maker of vampires was the end game all along. You must understand that his blood is more powerful than a thousand vampires combined. Powerful enough to overpower almost any attack in the blink of an eye. Quinn is now in possession of some of that blood and has ingested enough to overpower the entire convoy."

Jenny returned with Olivia snuggled on her hip in her pajamas as he spoke the terrifying words. She moved quickly across the room to Nora's bedroom, getting the small girl out of earshot of the frightening conversation.

"How the hell does something like that happen? Again, I ask you: how can one brand-new little vampire take on all of you? Are you kidding me? You're supposed to be these mighty beings, and Nora's dippy aunt can do what? Take the world down? You guys are useless!" Ezra's anger pushed him to get in the face of a demon. One that probably seemed a lot less powerful in that moment before the room began to rumble. A heat built around Elijah that pushed Ezra back a step and then another.

"Mr. Davis, do not push me!" Elijah's voice reverberated against the windowpanes, rattling the glass to a pinprick before breaking. The intense increase in temperature began to lick away any drop of moisture in the air. Nora blinked her eyes against the burning sensation, her lungs closing tightly, "This is beyond the scope of mortals. Your fears and needs hardly matter when the aumbry has been breached!" Elijah stood firmly as his dark pupils glowed with deep-set flames. The energy that reverberated from him made his elegant and controlled body seem to take up more space in the room than there was to occupy.

As quickly as he had erupted, the room went silent. Elijah and the three fae were the only ones that stood unaffected in the aftermath of his burst of anger. The others doubled over, swallowing gasp after gasp of the now-cooled air, struggling to steady themselves. Olivia's frightened cry from the bedroom was the only other sound.

Elijah closed his eyes, his body rigid yet calm. When he looked at them again, the anger in his eyes melted into agitation and then concern, "I am so very sorry for that. I understand how this must look to you. However, accusations of ineptitude or weakness are sorely misplaced and deeply inappropriate given the circumstances," he paused to clear his throat, "That being said, we are entering a situation that has come about due to grave errors. Errors that will be corrected and eliminated when the time comes," he spoke steadily and deliberately which exhibited more of the rage he held than his words did.

"Elijah, I..." Ezra attempted to get the words of apology out, contrition wrapped in fear stopping him before Elijah continued.

"No, I understand your frustration. I do apologize, truly. You have been locked away as a symptom of a situation we did not take seriously, and now I must rectify all aspects of that mistake. I have underestimated so many threats and..." he paused again, the tip of his tongue tracing the corner of his lips while he collected his thoughts, "Alliances are being made outside of our powers that have culminated in a dangerous situation for everyone. I will admit to our arrogance and give you my word that we will not push you aside any further simply because you are human. You, in turn, must understand that this is far beyond anything you could imagine. Your safety is still important to us. Unfortunately, you are no longer a priority, and for that, I am sorry. I will do what I can for you both," he turned to Jenny, "for you all. My hands are now tied as to what that may be now. I will do everything I can to correct all of the errors that have occurred under my watch."

They all stood in the silence that followed Elijah's admission until the three fae turned on their heels and threw open the door. Norman was standing on the other side in the dim hallway.

"What's going on?" he asked, his shy eyes scanning the gathered group and settling on Elijah.

"I...um...are you ok? I think there was an earthquake or something. Are you ok?" Nora lied, shuffling quickly to the door to slide in front of the glamor guards.

Norman's eyes would not leave Elijah's. He did not speak a word. The demon stood in the center of the apartment, stone-faced, apart from a small, polite smile.

"Maybe you should go check on Gail? Maybe you guys could go help him check on *Gail?*" Nora pushed, gesturing to the black-suited crew who lined the wall of her apartment, "Make sure the, uh, *earthquake* didn't damage anything down there."

Olivia appeared at the bedroom door beside her mom, her hands wiping away tears when she saw the newcomer, "Norman!" She ran to him and wrapped her arms around his leg. He reached down automatically and put his palm softly on her head, protectively.

"What's going on, Livey? What was that? Are you okay?" he questioned quickly, looking down at her with concern and then back to Elijah and the group with contempt in place of his usual shyness.

"Yeah. Are you?" Olivia asked, calming down with the comfort of her friend's arrival.

"I think they're right. It was an earthquake, Norman. It scared us, too," Jenny said, nervously looking at Elijah, who still stood with a small smile for the newcomer.

"Well, I think we should go check on Gail," Norman said flatly. He took Olivia by the hand, and they left without a word, with Jenny trailing them down the stairs.

Nora felt like they should all stick together if Quinn was such a threat, but having the little girl and the clueless shut-in away from an angry demon seemed more important at the moment. There was a bit of relief when two of the crew joined the parade down to Gail's.

"Well, that did not go as smoothly as I had hoped," Elijah said with a stiffly forced chuckle, "As it stands now, you will all remain here until sunrise. In the light of day, we will decide our next steps," he spoke as he started towards the door for the quick exit that was his way, but stopped himself, "I give you my word that I will let you know what is relevant going further. When I am able." He gave an awkward nod, turning again for the door and then back to them as if he had more to say, "Right. Okay. I will speak to you in the morning," he said with a tense sigh and was gone.

Not that he hadn't promised to keep them in the loop before. These were words he had spoken in the past. Even still, Nora knew that he was doing his best with them, even if he was not being open with them. Elijah had taken to being fond of his new human charges, and Nora hoped that feeling remained in light of the latest devastation that Quinn had caused. Being a human was clearly the lowest link on the chain in the eyes of the paranormal beings. Being human and the blood relative of the vampire causing the chaos they were facing had to make her even less. It would be another long night of waiting for sunrise, just as she had struggled through the night of the raid on Jude's house. The night she had staked him to save Ezra. This time Quinn was easily just as vengeful but now had the blood of the most powerful vampire in the universe surging through her veins.

No big deal, right?

Nora rubbed at her throbbing head and wished she hadn't smashed the fancy wine. It was going to be the longest night of her life yet.

CHAPTER FIVE

The evening took its time turning into the morning. The crew they had come to know – Melissa, Rowan, Zeke, and Davina – sadly let Nora and Ezra know they would no longer be on site with them. All hands on deck were being called for securing the aumbry and the main offices. The newest hires, the ones with the least experience, would be replacing them. Nora told an apologetic Melissa that it was better than nothing. It was frightening to be left behind, even though Elijah had told them that there were more significant threats to deal
with.

Ezra was taken down to his apartment to gather his necessities. He was officially moved up to Nora's in order to make it easier for the new agents to monitor their safety. Nora was disappointed that the faces that had become her new normal would no longer be around, and it felt like a loss of friendships even though they were just being reassigned jobs. The crew had become a symbol of safety and calm during their lockdown; now, when things seemed the most dangerous, they would be gone. Replaced by people so new that it had to be assumed they would be as qualified as Nora and Ezra were to keep themselves safe.

As the minutes felt like hours, they mostly sat silently on the couch, the television on low to keep an ear out for any sound that seemed out of the ordinary.

Just catch her again, and we are out of here.

Nora repeated that new mantra over and over in her head to stay calm until the glow of the sun crested behind the window blinds. Rowan returned with the two new members that were low enough on the list to be stuck with them.

"I'm just a text away, Nora. I may not be able to answer right away, but know that I'm here for you still. As best I can be," Rowan reminded her.

Nora pushed down how much she would miss him popping by every morning.

Their replacements seemed to be eager yet wound far too tightly. Jack was a baby-faced man in his early twenties. His crew-cut blonde hair was freshly shorn, and his bright green eyes were hyper-alert, constantly scanning. Belinda was taller than Jack by a few inches, her broad shoulders as stiff as the tight bun her chestnut hair was twisted into at the base of her neck.

"You look after these guys, all right? They're as good as one of us," Rowan said, giving Jack a firm clap on the shoulder before rushing out of the apartment with the rest of the crew.

Just like that, they were gone. Nora and Ezra looked over their new first line of defense. The fresh-out-of-the-academy-type stances did nothing to ebb their fears.

"So, how is this going to work? Are you going to be staying here as well?" Nora asked, wondering where everyone would find a place to sleep. Her apartment was larger than her old studio, but it had just one bed, one couch, and one armchair, and she knew that Silas would not be giving up his fur-covered chair.

"We'll be stationed downstairs, ma'am. We've been instructed not to leave the building, as have you," Belinda advised in a very flat, militant voice.

"At least not much has changed for *us* then," Ezra said with a tired, forced laugh.

A knock on the door had the new arrivals on their toes. Jack grabbed a silver-tipped stake from an obviously new holster strapped to his thigh and held it out comically as if it were a sword. Back to the wall, Belinda reached out to grab the incoming interloper when the knob turned to open. Nora had never felt less at ease with her own safety.

"What the hell?" Jenny shouted as she was snatched by her shirt and dragged into the room. Sarah stood behind in the hallway, confusion twisting her face.

"Belinda! Let her go!" Nora ordered, palming her head in frustration. Not a good start.

Ezra released an exasperated sigh and tossed himself on his worn spot on the couch, "Elijah won't even consider me for a position, and these aces are supposed to protect us?"

"Who are you?" Jack demanded, still holding the stake out.

"This is Jenny! It's her building!" Nora shouted, pushing Belinda's hand away from her friend.

"Seems like something you should already know, don't you think?" Ezra snorted.

"Why was this door unlocked?" Belinda demanded, ushering Sarah in and shutting the door.

"Probably because you didn't lock it after the crew left. When you were standing right beside it," Ezra said without looking at her, slumping down and flicking the remote through the viewing options. Sarah took the seat beside him, looking around at everyone, trying to sort out what had just happened.

"Yes, well...as long as these guests are okay by you, we'll go down and get set up," Belinda turned away, hiding the flush that crept up her neck to her cheeks, "Jack! Let's go."

Jack stepped out of his on-guard stance and holstered his shiny new stake to follow her to the door. He turned to them with a serious face, "Lock this behind us."

They headed down the stairs, arguing quietly with each other about protocols.

When she closed and locked the door behind the bumbling two, Nora shook her head. If they didn't catch Quinn soon, there was a good chance these two would end up sticking a stake in her chest if she entered a room too quickly. She double-checked the locks, more to keep the new crew members out than supernatural threats.

"What the hell was that all about?" Jenny asked, pointing towards where they had just stood, "*That's* who Elijah thinks can keep us all safe?"

"It seems with everything taking a turn for the worse and becoming far more dangerous, they only had a couple of Keystone Cops left to be in charge of protecting us," Nora said, scrubbing the fatigue from her face with her hands, "Lucky us, huh?"

"Seriously? They're going to be the ones looking after this building?" Jenny asked, slack-jawed.

"They're going to be in the building. How much they'll look after, I can't say," Nora grumbled.

With that grim outlook, Jenny quickly made plans with Sarah to get the coven together to see what more they could do to keep the building secured. Knowing that the trusted crew they had was gone, she immediately went downstairs to get Olivia. With the change in security, she said she would keep Olivia on her heel until it all blew over, even when the sun was up. Nora liked how sure she was that it would be over sooner rather than later because, at the moment, she wasn't. She would trust the opinion of a woman who had been in the middle of Aumbry Valley drama for much longer than she had or that she planned to be.

"So, you're staying here full-time now?" Sarah asked Ezra when Jenny headed downstairs.

"Those are the orders. Next, they'll make the three of us lock ourselves in the closet," Ezra quipped with a shake of his head.

"We'd be pretty cramped in there," Sarah replied, looking at Nora.

"Yeah, it would be," he gave an awkward laugh, "With you in there, too, for sure!" Ezra looked to Nora and continued when Sarah turned a quizzical look to him,

"The three I meant was Nora, Silas, and me," he shifted in his seat, "I mean, luckily you aren't on any kind of lockdown, and can come and go."

"Oh, for sure. Of course," Sarah covered her discomfort with a wave of her hand and a quick laugh, "I can't imagine how this has been for you."

"Yeah. One good thing is I'm guessing it's not going to be a big deal for us to leave soon if they have bigger fish to fry," Ezra said with crossed fingers.

"I bet they don't want you to go," Sarah replied, eyes on Ezra, "I mean, they'll probably insist you stay, Nora. Your connection to Quinn probably makes you pretty important to them," Sarah said to her, rifling around in the sling bag she wore, "At least until they catch her. Then I'm sure you can't wait to get out of here."

"I can't be that important to them if they have dumb and dumber watching over us," Nora said, putting on the third pot of coffee of the day.

"Maybe that's the point," Sarah said and took out a heavy-looking glass ball from a velvet satchel, "Maybe they want Quinn to be able to get to you."

Nora did not like that idea when Ezra mentioned it and was even more uncomfortable about it with the new lack of protection. It was not like it would be her first time being bait. Although, there had been no intention of letting Quinn get her hands on her the last time. This could be a *two-birds, one-stone* situation that would clear up the loose ends of Quinn and Jude's mess. That would explain the incompetence that was presently taking up residence in her old apartment.

"They wouldn't do that to her," Ezra said, sitting up at attention.

"Do what? Bait Quinn with her? You know they have and certainly will again. If they're off-put by mortal witches, you can only imagine how little they think of powerless humans. The only power Nora has is her connection to Quinn. You can be sure they'll bleed that until it's no longer of use."

The hair on Nora's neck stood up at the use of *bleed* to describe her use.

"If that's the case, why don't we just leave? Find a car and get the hell away from here. If Quinn is breaking into the aumbry and stealing magic blood and shit, I highly doubt she still cares about us. That crazy bitch is looking to do something bigger than us. For real, she doesn't need to do something that extreme to get to us. Nora, we should do it. We should just leave," Ezra said, standing quickly, "This could be our chance."

Nora liked the idea of running as far away from the nightmares the valley held. Unfortunately, her feet were frozen in place. How far would they have to go to be far enough away? Did that distance even exist? She told herself that she would stop blindly obeying the orders being put upon her, but she felt herself wanting to still hide away in the pseudo-safety of Dunhope Manor.

Sarah turned to Nora, "I don't think heading out right away to places unknown is the right answer, guys. I think you both should stay put for now, at least, until we know a little more about what's going on. The coven may have some ideas. We may even find a way to get you somewhere else safely. It would be best if you gave us all time. You need to trust us," she held up the shining ball she had retrieved from her purse, "This isn't much, but I want you to have it."

Nora stared at the dark sphere when Sarah approached her and placed it in her palm. It was cold and smooth in her hand, and her fingers almost felt as if they sunk into the uneven surface when she gripped it, "What is this for?"

"It's an obsidian ball. It's a crystal made from hardened lava that helps clear negativity and can give you clarity in courage," she took Nora's hand and the crystal into her own hands, "Keep it near you at all times. I mean it. At all times. Every little thing can help right now."

"Oh, wow. Thanks, Sarah," Nora looked at their reflections in the ball and then smiled at her for the kind gesture. They had not had a chance to get to know each other well, so the effort was greatly appreciated.

Jenny gave a quick, shy grin, "I should head down and give Jenny a hand. When I know what we're doing, we'll let you know," she said to Ezra, "There's no way that we're going to let those boobs downstairs run the show. This is Jenny's building, and I know she'll protect it."

Nora twisted the locks on the door when she left and stared at the obsidian ball in her hand. She felt no different holding it, and the apartment felt no less negative. It *was* relaxing to turn it over in her hands. The soothing cool of the surface stilled her mind.

"Tell me you don't believe in that crap," Ezra said through a yawn as he poured two mugs of coffee.

"Believe in what?" Nora didn't look up from the stone.

"Crystals and chakras and all that crap."

"I think the only crap right now is not being open to anything. If there's one thing I can do right now, after what we've been through in the past few months, is believe in anything and everything," Nora proclaimed. She would take any help she could get.

"There has to be a line, Nor. A rock isn't going to change anything except by being shiny and pretty."

"I have no idea what will help, but I'm not going to turn down anything at this point. Hell, silver can kill vampires, fae blood can completely heal humans, and rocks are the unbelievable line?" Nora frowned.

Ezra held the coffee out to her, "Supernatural things and rocks are completely different."

Nora didn't notice the mug, her eyes watching the ball turn over in her palms, "Well, maybe these are just supernatural rocks. Then would you believe that they can affect us?"

"I'll admit that they seem to have the power to make us fight, so that's something," he set the mug on the counter in front of her when she did not take it and grabbed the salt shaker, "Not much good at getting rid of negative energy then, is it? Maybe we should use this magical salt?"

Nora growled with frustration, "Fine, I'll put it in my room, so you won't have to think about it. And just so you know, salt does have a special power. Just ask Jenny...or your little friend Sarah!" she snapped over her shoulder as she stomped into her room and pulled open her top dresser drawer.

As she placed it on top of a pile of t-shirts, the hairs on the back of her neck stirred when she felt eyes on her. A flash of movement in the corner of her vision had her turning quickly. Her eyes adjusted to the lower light of her room when she tried to focus on the corner where she was sure she saw a smoky fog linger for a moment and disappear. Blinking, she found nothing but her hamper.

"Ez, can you come in here?" she called out with a shaky voice.

She stood in place as his footfalls could be heard crossing the apartment to her room, "What's wrong? Did the crystal say something crazy?" He stopped beside her when he saw her staring at the corner of her room, his mood turning serious, "What is it? What happened?"

"Do you see anything over there?" Nora asked, even though she could no longer see the mist that she wasn't even sure had been there.

Ezra took a moment to look before answering, "No, what am I looking for? Your dirty clothes?"

Nora shook her head and rubbed her eyes, "I thought I saw a...I saw...," She exhaled with frustration, "I don't know. I'm just overtired and more than a little overwhelmed, I guess."

"We should try and get some sleep. I'm thinking we're not going to be getting any updates any time soon," Ezra sighed, giving Nora a strained smile, "I guess we're officially roomies now."

A soft but persistent knock started on the front door.

"Who is it now?" Ezra asked the universe and headed to the door. Looking through the peephole, he could find anyone in the hall until a little mess of brown curls backed up into view. Twisting the locks and opening the door, they found Olivia smiling up at them.

"Hi, Norma! Hi Ezra!" she chirped as she pushed passed them into the apartment, "Mom's doing work stuff with Sarah. Can I hang out here?" She popped herself up on a stool at the kitchen island.

"Sweetie, you know you're always welcome here, but does your mom know you're up here? I think she wants you with her today," Nora said, automatically pulling out one of the juice boxes for her.

"She's busy with *Sarah*," she replied with an adorable little eye roll. She spoke the name as if it was cooties incarnate.

She worried that Jenny did not know she had left her apartment and squatted down, so they were eye to eye, "I still think she wants you downstairs with her, even if she's busy."

"I don't wanna. I don't like Sarah. She's bossy," Olivia sneered, fighting the straw into the juice box.

Nora softly scolded her when Ezra only laughed, "Aw, that's not nice to say, Olivia. Sarah is a nice girl."

"Nope. Don't like her," Olivia grinned widely when she finally popped the straw into the juice, "Norman is busy with Gail, and the Dancing Girl is already asleep."

"The dancing girl?" Ezra asked.

"It's her...*friend*. We can't see her," Nora answered under her breath.

"Oh, god, don't tell me we have ghosts now, too?" he moaned, looking about the room's shadows. Nora was happy that he came to the same first conclusion she had. Even with Jenny's reassurance, she joined him in scanning the room.

"She's not a ghost, silly. She's a little girl like me. But she lives in the ballroom upstairs," Olivia cheerfully told him before taking a big slurp from the straw.

Jenny's muffled voice called from the hallway as she banged on the door. Nora moved quickly to open it for the panicked mother.

"She's here; she's okay," Nora stepped out of the way.

"Baby, I told you not to leave the apartment without me!" Jenny panted and hauled the little girl up into her arms.

Olivia squirmed until she could reach her juice box again, "I didn't leave. I'm just up here."

Jenny hugged her tightly, "I don't want you out of my sight, okay?"

The girl's lip trembled when she noticed the frantic state of her mother, "I didn't want to bug you when you're doing work, so I came to see my friends. I'm sorry."

"It's okay, baby. I'm not mad. I was just worried," Jenny soothed and kissed her daughter's head.

"Norman and her dancing ghost friend were busy, apparently," Ezra said, tossing a pillow and blanket onto the couch.

"She's not a ghost!" Olivia insisted.

"Olivia, did you say she lives in the ballroom upstairs?" Nora asked and gave a concerned look to Jenny. The ballroom was rundown and dangerous for anyone, let alone for a small child running around.

"Yeah, she lets me visit sometimes." The little girl turned guilty eyes to her mother when she realized what she had admitted.

"You haven't been going up there, have you?" Jenny asked, her voice stern.

"I'm sorry, mommy. She's so lonely there. She's not supposed to leave, so I have to keep her company up there," Olivia whimpered.

"Yeah, awesome. That's a ghost. Awesome. Ghosts now. Perfect," Ezra muttered to no one in particular.

Olivia furrowed her brow and crossed her arms with annoyance, "She's not a ghost, Ezra! I'm just the only one allowed to see her."

Nora stepped towards her, "Why don't you stay here with Ezra, and mommy and I will go and make sure she's okay?" she asked the little girl and turned to Ezra, "We'll go make sure there aren't any big bad ghosts up there and get it locked up. The fewer ways in and out of here, the better."

"Shouldn't you have the two downstairs handle that?" Ezra asked, clearly not wanting to check it out himself.

"The less I have to deal with those two, the better, and this is my building. My house," Jenny said, setting Olivia down beside him.

Ezra just shrugged and turned on the TV to find cartoons for the little girl. They were on their own now and had to step up and take charge. The mist she saw crept into her thoughts, and she hoped that Jenny was right when she said that there were no ghosts residing at Dunhope Manor. With the sun high in the sky, she was at least sure there wasn't a threat of vampires jumping out at her up there. She and Jenny moved up the stairs to the fourth floor in synchronized steps.

The dust that should have rested in front of the entrance to the ballroom had been worn away with Olivia's little footprints. Nora was glad that the little girl had not been harmed with what looked like many trips to the decaying floor of the manor. Not that she could blame her. The one thing she did adore about growing up in her parents' expansive brownstone was exploring the nooks and crannies when adult eyes were not around, and she could let her imagination take her on adventures.

Jenny easily opened the door and her lips twisted into a frustrated frown when she found the door was not locked, "She must have found the keys I have in the cupboard. I had this locked up months ago."

They entered the decrepit room slowly and silently as if there was a chance that they would catch a little ghost girl spinning in dance on the ballroom floor. The vaulted ceiling, which rose at least fifteen feet above them, was crisscrossed by enormous, solid wooden beams. It gave a glimpse into how impressive the room once was in its glamourous heyday when Jude owned it before he was turned into a vampire. A chill that wasn't in the air tickled Nora's back when she pictured him holding court where she stood.

The room was mostly empty, with large chunks of the mosaic hardwood floor rotting away. The large section of the wall that most likely held a grand stained glass window had been covered over with a sheet of pressboard that itself was starting to rot. Pieces of the long-ago lost window sat swept against the wall below, under a thick coating of dust.

"I can't believe she's been coming up here," Jenny fumed. She carefully walked to a corner that had been cleaned of dust and debris. A fuzzy pink blanket had been spread out picnic style, and a selection of dolls had been lined up against the wall. A larger doll sat in front of them with a tutu and ballet slippers. Jenny picked it up and turned to show Nora, "Do you think this could be the dancing girl she's going on about?"

Looking about the room and the few pieces of furniture that still had dust covers tossed over, she didn't see anything else out of the ordinary. Her courage was quickly depleting at the thought of looking under the dust covers or behind anything that was casting shadows. She shrugged to Jenny and found herself stepping back towards the door, "It could be. It's not unusual for a kid to have imaginary friends. Especially a kid as creative as Olivia."

"I guess. We put a lot of charms on this building to keep things from getting in, so the odds that it's anything else does seem unlikely. Unfortunately, unlikely things aren't so unlikely in Aumbry Valley," Jenny mused, gathering up the dolls into the blanket and slinging it over her shoulder, "I'll get this place locked up and boarded in a bit. Just the musty air alone has to be bad for her little lungs."

They stepped into the hallway and started down the stairs after shutting the door to the creepy room behind them.

"Jenny, if Jude could get in here, what are the chances that Quinn could?"

"Pretty much zero unless she's invited in," Jenny said calmly, as if Nora was asking about the weather forecast.

"But she was with Jude. They were a couple. Does that give her rights or anything to what was his?" Nora pressed.

"It doesn't work like that, luckily. It's not a matter of rights or paperwork with them. It's the essence of ownership, like a royal title or something. It's passed on or lost to time. When Jude owned the place, yeah, any vampire could have entered if he allowed it. Which pisses me off that I didn't know, but now that he died, all supernatural ownership to the property is dead and gone, just like him."

Nora felt queasy at the memory of him turning to ash at her hand, "Oh. That's good," she said softly but not convincingly.

Jenny noticed the darkness that had cast itself over her friend's face, "Sorry. I guess that was insensitive."

"It's okay. I'm just trying to get used to all of this. I guess I'm trying to decide if I *want* to get used to all of this."

"That's totally understandable. I've been here since, oh god, it's got to be ten years now. We moved when Mark inherited the building, and it's all just become normal to me," Jenny said as she stepped into the hallway for the third floor and Nora's apartment, "I thought we would leave after he, well, when he...," she pursed her lips, stopping herself from going further about her husband's death, "Anyways, it just became home. Having my coven here sort of makes it that way."

Nora wanted to press further to discover how Jenny's husband's death came about, but tact overcame curiosity. If Jenny wanted her to know, she knew that she would tell her.

"It looks like that coven is going to be our best bet to keep ourselves safe now that we've been pushed aside by the Firm," Nora offered instead of prying.

"Yeah. They're all coming by later to set some plans in place. Hopefully, the two newbies from the bureau crew don't get in our way," Jenny laughed and followed Nora into her apartment.

Ezra and Olivia were deep into a discussion on the merits of one cartoon over another, neither of which Nora had ever even heard of. Olivia stopped and gave her mother a guilty pout when she saw the filled blanket slung over her shoulder. Jenny gave a jerk of her head to gesture for her to follow her home.

"But mom...," Olivia started to plead.

"No '*but mom*,' missy. We need to have a little talk," Jenny responded, holding her free hand out for the little girl to take.

Olivia's lip jutted out in protest when she shuffled over to follow her mother, "It's not fair."

"Well, that's life, little lady. Best get used to it," Jenny said, giving Olivia's curls a ruffle before she took her hand, "You guys try to get some sleep. You both look like hell," she said matter-of-factly and headed for the stairs.

Nora locked the door behind her and crumpled on the couch beside Ezra.

He tossed an arm over the back of the couch and turned his attention to her, "So, any ghosts or ghouls up there?"

Nora snorted, "No, just a lot of dust and mold."

"That's good, I guess," Ezra laughed. He laid back to snuggle his head on his pillow and kicked his legs over Nora's.

"What are we going to do now, Ez? I feel like we're sitting ducks."

"We've been sitting ducks since we arrived in this bonkers town, Nor. The only thing that's changed is that we don't have skilled guards locking us down. The patients can run the asylum now," he laughed and tugged his blanket up.

"How are you so chill about this?"

"I'm not chill. I'm just taking it as it comes now, and I'm not going to make any good decision this tired. The sun is up, so we're as safe as we're going to get," he yawned and fluffed the pillow under his head, "I'm going to get some sleep, and then we're going to come up with our next move. Whether we're leaving, or staying, or anything in between."

"We can't just leave," Nora said, chewing nervously on her thumbnail.

Ezra lifted his head, a look of humor set on his face, "Why? The bumbling duo downstairs going to stop us?"

Nora turned her head, "Elijah told us to stay here."

"Nora, when are you going to admit to yourself that the demon who used us as vamp bait doesn't give a shit about us. Especially now that he's left us, like you said, as sitting ducks."

"I just think...," Nora started, unable to decide what she thought. She knew Ezra was right.

"I just think, you either shush for now, or I'm going to take that bed of yours so I can get some good sleep."

Nora frowned and pushed his legs off of her lap, "Fine. We'll talk later."

She shuffled into her room as the fatigue from the lessening adrenaline took hold, and the sleepless nights started to catch up with her. Some rest would be the best first step toward whatever was to come. She stared at her ceiling, waiting for the creaks of the old floor to start sounding like footsteps. She fell into a deep sleep before she could hear a thing.

CHAPTER SIX

The few hours of sleep she was able to attain did help her mind slow the what-ifs just a bit. The body buzz of fatigue still zipped along every one of her nerve endings, begging for more time in bed when she dragged her eyes open. She decided that she would double down on what Ezra had said and hoped it would get her through until she knew what would happen next. What Quinn was up to had to be bigger than her, than Quinn's desire for revenge. There was no way that she would be causing such a raucous within the Aumbry Valley higher-ups just to get even with her for the loss of Jude. The Quinn she met after she had been turned was no longer the woman she had grown up with, and there was still a chance that there was enough of the flighty, non-comital gal left of her to move on from Jude. Just as she had all of her other past one-true loves of the moment, Nora could be yet another forgotten person in her ever-changing life. A year ago, that would have broken her heart. Now, it was the best that Nora could hope
for.

Leaving could be a possibility. They would be one less responsibility for Elijah to worry about, which would have to be a relief for him with the stress he had been under. Even though there was no way to know what her future would hold, it was nice to feel like she was taking back some control. Where to go seemed less important than when to go. Looking at the clock, she saw it was mid-afternoon. No matter her decision, there wouldn't be time to pack up and hit the road. It would have to wait until the next day at the earliest anyways. She threw a pillow over the clock and tried to scrub the sleep from her face. Not having a regular schedule and sleeping only when she got a chance would not work for her for much longer. Patting around the bed in search of Silas, she found herself alone. He was probably on the couch curled up on his new BFF Ezra.

She stretched out in bed, her fingers and toes pushing as far as her body would let her when a woman's giggle from within the apartment had Nora sitting straight up, alert. Another sing-song laugh had her out of bed and moving to her door. Ezra's returning laughter brought relief when she realized it was just Sarah. She debated whether to stay put and give them some privacy. Her bladder won the argument, and she tip-toed out of her room.

"Hey, Nora. Did you manage to get any sleep?" Sarah asked when Nora emerged.

Nora stopped in place, pressing down her tangled bedhead, "Yeah. Not enough, but better than nothing."

"Says the one with the bed and not the lumpy couch," Ezra said, flipping the strips of bacon he was preparing on the stove.

"Fair enough," Nora nodded. She slipped into the bathroom to freshen up before joining them in the kitchen. The cold coffee pot was filled with sludgy remains, and she frowned, pouring it into the sink before starting another pot. There had been more caffeine consumption since they had been on lockdown than in all of the time she had dragged herself up and out to the temp jobs she had before meeting Elijah. Thinking of all of the spots she had worked, she turned to Sarah, "So, do all of the jobs around here have to go through the temp agency? I know Ezra and I both had to find work that way."

"The ones in the know, if you know what I mean, don't. They have it set up to handle the normies that find their way here. The ones that they don't want to know about their secrets. It seems to work. Most people who end up here have their own secrets they're leaving behind and are happy to keep their heads down and live their lives."

"Why would they want to have them around? Wouldn't they want people who didn't have to be on guard with their secrets all the time? Couldn't they just do the vampire influence on them to control their minds or something?" Nora wondered, knowing those secrets had not made her life any easier.

"Who the hell would want to put up with supernatural nonsense for minimum wage knowingly?" Ezra remarked, making Sarah laugh.

"There's that for sure, and there are some that have been influenced, I'm sure. The temp agency is also a good way to keep tabs on them. They also like to have the labor and the other uses that they have," Sarah shook her head when Ezra and Nora looked at her with scrunched noses, "No, not vamp food. Well, not all of them. You know they already have people for that.

There are a lot more beings here than just vampires, guys."

Nora didn't dare let her mind roam to all of the options, "Yeah, I guess. It's all just so weird to me. You grew up here, didn't you?"

"Yup, I'm a lifer," she grinned, trying to take a too-hot piece of bacon from Ezra's tongs. It dropped back into the pan, and she gave an apologetic shrug when the grease popped, "Even still, I get what you're saying. It never really feels normal here. It's a lot all the time."

"That's an understatement," Ezra bemoaned. He put the tongs down and stretched while rubbing his lower back. He groaned and looked to Nora, "What would you think if I moved some stuff around out here to make room for my bed?"

"Do you think you'll be up here long enough to bother with that?" Sarah asked, pulling out a carton of eggs. Nora wasn't sure how she felt about her being so comfortable in her kitchen as she watched her crack the eggs into a pan. Her pan.

"I don't know, probably not, but I don't want to rely on that couch anymore," Ezra scoffed.

Sarah looked around the room and back to him with a questioning tilt of her head, "You were just saying that you don't think Elijah cares what you do, and you're going to follow his rules still? Seems dumb to me. You should be able to move into your old apartment at the very least. It's not like those two lumps downstairs are going to do much. Better yet, get your own place again. You've got the money in the bank for it."

Nora was surprised that Sarah would have such a strong opinion of Ezra's living situation. She watched Sarah playfully toss a kitchen towel to him before opening the fridge to pull out the milk and give Ezra a little bump with her hip when she passed. Sarah's feelings were on full display, and they were much stronger than Nora had noticed. The flirtations of days before were becoming a full-on attempt to domesticate with him in Nora's own kitchen. She felt like she was intruding and didn't like it. Ezra, as usual, seemed to take no notice of Sarah's intentions.

"I dunno. I'm kind of used to here now. It seems as good as any place for the time we have left in this crazy town. Even before last night when they told me I had to be, I liked it here," he said, smiling at Nora. He pulled down three plates from the cupboard, "I'm pretty sure it's the nicest place in the building. Nicer than mine, that's for sure, and no crazy, chirping birds screaming through the walls."

Sarah put a hand on her hip, biting her lip before she pressed again, "What about getting your own place, then? You loved that house you were fixing up, and you just let them talk you into moving."

"To be fair, we had both just killed a couple of vamps and possibly had Nora's crazy aunt after us. Listening to Damper Demon Elijah and his sidekick seemed the best idea," Ezra shrugged, "Anyways, I'm not going to the bother of finding a new place here if we don't even know if we're staying. If I were to get a place of my own, it's not going to be in this crazy town. Fool me once, man."

Nora laughed at how his eyes widened, and he held his hands up in defeat. They had spent many an evening discussing what their lives would be if they hadn't made their way to the valley. At least she had come on her own. Gabriel's mind meddling had been the reason for Ezra's arrival. She considered that his involvement in getting him there could be another reason Ezra had such negative feelings for him and could see his point on that one if it was true.

"What about joining one of the crews? I thought that's what you still wanted," Sarah proposed, taking the plates from him to set on the table.

"If I *have* to stay, I could see that. I just don't know. We seem to have some options finally," Ezra nodded hopefully to Nora.

"Having Quinn on the loose again doesn't give us *a lot* of options. It just seems like we may have the chance to get out of here without being watched 24/7, and I don't think joining the BITN crew will help you move on, Ez. I think you might go all Helsing and make everything worse," Nora laughed.

"It's Van Helsing, not Helsing, and that's just a story," Sarah snapped, pointing the plate she held at Nora, "and maybe that's not the worse thing for him. He has every right to hate them. It's not like they're easy to love."

Nora's brow raised at the change of mood that Sarah had turned on her.

Ezra picked up the tongs again to grab the overcooked bacon, "Whatever I feel about them doesn't matter right now," he turned to Nora, "What do you think? Should we hit the road or give it a few days?"

The question that seemed to be asked more than answered.

"I don't think you understand how the Firm works, guys. Just because you think they're not watching you anymore doesn't mean they're not. Trust me. You want to stick around, for now, to see how this plays out. Just because you leave the valley doesn't mean that the valley will let you stay away," Sarah plucked a piece of bacon from the plate and popped it in her mouth with a crunch, "I thought your family owned a breakfast restaurant? This is greasy charcoal!"

"They owned it. I ate there. I never said I *could* cook. I said I *would* cook," Ezra grabbed the bacon slice from her and popped it in his mouth, "This isn't so bad," he said between loud crunches.

"She's right, Ezra. About staying put and the bacon," Nora teased, "We're getting too excited and ahead of ourselves. It's only been a few hours. According to Elijah, we're still supposed to stay in the apartment. Quinn is still out there doing god knows what to god knows who with the power of the greatest vampire of all time surging through her crazy, hippy blood. I want out of here just as much as you do. Having things worse for the supes than for us gives us a window to, but that doesn't mean it has to be immediately. We need a plan, and it wouldn't hurt to follow the rules for a little while more. It may help them forget about us if we stay off their radar."

"Says the girl who traipsed up to a spooky and unknown part of the building right after being told that?" Ezra accused with a crooked grin, "You're already living like the rules don't apply anymore."

Nora frowned, "That's different."

Ezra's jaw dropped playfully, "Ha! No, it's not."

"Yes, it is. It's not leaving the building or moving miles away, so it's different," Nora countered. She pulled out forks when he started to dish the food onto plates. Her stomach rumbled at the scent of the simple yet overcooked meal.

"I think we should wait and see what Jenny says. She's meeting with the Elders now, and I'm sure with all they've done for you guys, you should at least wait to hear what they think," Sarah said, stopping the back and forth between the two.

Nora agreed with that point. The coven, most of whom they had never met, had worked on charms and spells to keep them safe. It seemed obvious to assume that they would step up to keep Jenny and Olivia from harm. The worry was that stepping in to keep Nora and Ezra safe could also put them at odds with some very nasty vampires and who-knows-what other beings who could be involved with Quinn. They were hoping for strangers to help fight their personal battle, and she was thankful. As much as Nora knew they needed their help, she hated pulling more people into their messy fold. The least she could do was wait to hear what they thought the next move should be.

"Is Jenny the boss of your group? Your, what's it called?" Ezra swirled his fork in the air, thinking of the word, "the coven, is it?"

"No, that would be our High Priestess. Jenny is the coven's Maiden. She's like the right-hand man to our High Priestess. It's a very important position. She's held it almost since she arrived here," Sarah said with evident reverence.

"Was her husband a witch, too?" he asked, shoveling eggs into his mouth.

Nora stopped her fork halfway to her mouth when he asked. It seemed wrong to get information on Jenny's husband from anyone other than her, but if Sarah had anything she wanted to share, the inquisitor in Nora was begging to hear it.

"He was, and he wasn't. His father was an elder before he passed away. Mark grew up never wanting anything to do with it, even though he married another witch," Nora held her breath, hoping she would continue when Sarah stopped to nibble a piece of bacon, "When we were kids, he was big about rebelling against it all. I think that's why he moved away. But then he meets Jenny and ends up back here when his dad died, and he inherited this building."

"You grew up with her husband?" Ezra asked.

"Yeah, my family goes back generations here. Pretty much why you should listen to me when I say it's not that easy to leave," Sarah said with pursed lips and turned to Nora, "Unless you want to go after your aunt. I'm sure they'd be okay with that. Maybe she would turn you, and you could teach her how to be a decent being again. You know, decent like you."

Nora didn't know how to take that bit of a compliment and wondered where the sharp edge to Sarah's attitude was coming from. If it was over Ezra, she assumed Sarah was smart enough to know that she had no power over whether he chose to stay in the valley or not.

Before she could reply, Ezra cut in, "I doubt Nora wants anything to do with her, let alone be able to teach a vamp to be decent. No matter how awesome she is."

Sarah pressed a grin to her face and stood to bring her plate to the kitchen, "Yeah, I guess. Anyways, I need to get back down and see how it's going. Their meeting is probably over by now," Sarah added as she scraped her leftover food into the trash and set her dishes in the sink, "I'll let you guys know what they have to say. I'm sure they'll be including you in the next meeting. We aren't as secretive and dismissive of non-magic humans and mortals as the fae and demons," she said with a wink, "Speaking of which," she started to say.

"Which witch is which?" Ezra asked with a proud laugh at his joke.

"Yes, yes. That keeps getting funnier, fella," Sarah jeered to what must be an ongoing inside joke between them. She put her hands on his shoulders from behind where he sat, "Anyways, where is the obsidian I gave you, Nora? I want to refresh it."

"Oh, I put it in my room," Nora told her, not adding that it was because Ezra was making fun of it.

"You have to remember that you need to keep it close by for it to work, missy," Sarah playfully chided and nodded toward her room, "Can you grab it?"

Nora was having a tough time keeping up with Sarah's mood swings. She didn't know if it was a witch thing, a Sarah thing, or a reaction to the stress, but she knew Jenny certainly didn't have the ups and downs that she was discovering Sarah to possess. Either way, she did as she was asked and retrieved the stone from her drawer. Sarah took it from her and muttered unintelligible words over it, turning it over in her fingers before handing it back to her. Ezra was polite enough not to comment, even though he gave a look of disapproval to Nora.

Sarah pressed it to Nora's hand and held on for a quick moment, "You need to keep that in your pocket or very near to you for it to do any good."

"Why don't I get a magic rock to protect me?" Ezra mocked, unable to stay quiet.

"Because you don't have a crazy vamp aunt on the loose, do you?" she retorted with a laugh before quickly stopping herself, "I better go."

Without another word, she picked up her bag and was out the door. The citizens of Aumbry Valley were undoubtedly fans of a quick exit.

Nora moved to re-lock it with Sarah's up and down emotions still swirling about her, "What was that all about?"

"What?" Ezra asked, swiping a piece of toast from Nora's plate.

"Is it just me, or did she seem a little...I don't know, weird? Bitchy? I don't want to say that, but she was kind of bitchy to me, wasn't she?"

"She's a little on edge, but I think we all are. She was nice enough to sing to your magic rock."

Nora threw him an impatient glare, "I guess. I just felt like...I don't know. You know her better than I do. You would know your little girlfriend better than your roommate would. I'm probably just reading into it," Nora pointed out. She was caught off guard by the edge in her voice.

Was she jealous of Sarah? There was no way that she would be. Ezra was just her friend. Sarah's mood swings must have been contagious.

"Girlfriend? She is not my girlfriend, thank you very much," Ezra sneered.

Nora watched him take the other piece of toast from her plate, "Does she know that?"

"Is someone a little jealous of me having other friends? You don't see me saying anything about Rowan hanging around," Ezra wiped a napkin to his mouth, "Or, like, you know, Melissa always being here."

"Not that they will be anymore," Nora snapped. She looked at the crystal that Sarah had given her, wondering if it did have the power to affect anything. The light from the window picked up the deep green hue within the shiny surface when she held it up, "This is our protection now, I guess."

Ezra gave his head a shake as he rolled his eyes. He crumpled his napkin onto his plate and moved to the sink to wash up the dishes in silence. Nora put the stone in the pocket of her robe and headed for the bathroom to shower. She was getting grumpy and on edge, and a hot shower was the best solution she could think of. Maybe another nap, too, before the sunset alarms started ringing out. Movement in the corner of her eye had her head turning quickly to the far corner of the apartment.

"What?" Ezra asked, moving to her side when she gasped.

"I thought I saw...like a big swirl of smoke. It's what I thought I saw in my room."

Ezra followed her gaze and stared at the empty corner, "I think your eyes are playing tricks on you, Nor. There's nothing there."

Nora narrowed her eyes and agreed with him when she found nothing but the exposed brick wall. The feeling of being watched slowly faded, but the rattled nerves remained. The past few months had shown her that the impossible was, in fact, entirely possible. Seeing the same mist twice pointed to it being something more than just her tired eyes. She rubbed her fingers on the crystal in her pocket and headed to the bathroom.

"Don't take too long; I need in there," Ezra called through the closed door.

"Why don't you let me be and head over to your girlfriend's," Nora teased with a sour tone.

"She's *not* my girlfriend," Ezra barked back.

Nora laughed at the annoyance in his voice. He was so easy to get worked up. Her laugh caught in her throat when a cough that started as a tickle erupted, squeezing the breath from her lungs. The dry grip in her throat sprinted deeper into her chest until she was unable to draw in a breath. Her eyes welled with tears as she struggled to bang on the door, desperate for help. Grabbing onto the sink, her reflection in the mirror framed the horrifying state of her face. Spiders, the size of pinheads, covered her skin, scurrying across the surface, making their way into her mouth, her nose, and her eyes. She could see dozens of them overtaking her even though she could not feel a single one's microscopic legs shuffling about. Clawing at the invaders did nothing to keep them from infesting her and filling her throat. Stars appeared before her as the lack of oxygen smothered her into unconsciousness. She was out before she could feel her head hit the edge of the cold porcelain sink as she toppled to the floor, blood streaming from the gash.

CHAPTER SEVEN

Ezra's worried face blurred with the out-of-focus wall behind him when Nora came to. As he started to come into focus hazily, Nora reached up to swat at her face, feeling nothing and finding nothing on her hands but blood when Ezra grabbed her wrists to stop her from scratching violently at her skin.

"Get them off!" she screamed, struggling to free her hands from his grip, "Help me! Get them off!"

"Get what off? Nora, there's nothing there. Calm down!" he pleaded with her and released her arms to grab a towel for the blood that dripped down from above her temple, "Here, put this on your head. Nora, listen to me! You're bleeding. You need to put this on your head."

Nora scrambled up from the floor to the mirror above the sink. There were no spiders to be found on her head that now throbbed. She took the towel from Ezra's shaking hand and held it to her head, "What the hell was that?"

"Took the words right out of my mouth! What happened? I just heard you scream and then a huge bang. I'm guessing that was your head," he took the towel to look at the damage, wiping some of the blood away before taking Nora's hand and lifting it to hold it back in place. He rummaged through the closet for bandages and antiseptic.

Nora stared into the mirror, using a loose end of the towel to wipe away the blood that had dripped down to her chin, "I...there were spiders. I started to cough, and there were so many spiders."

"You freaked out that bad over some spiders?" Ezra looked around the small bathroom space in search of what frightened her, "It's an old house, Nor. You have to have seen spiders in here before."

"No, it wasn't just a regular spider. They were all over my face! They were crawling in my mouth," Nora touched her neck and lips, trying to piece together what was real. The pain and gash to her head sure were.

Ezra piled first aid supplies in the sink and took hold of the towel, "What are you talking about?" He looked her face over, looking for any sign of the invading arachnids.

"I swear I saw them. I couldn't breathe," Nora pulled the towel from his grip when Ezra led her out of the bathroom and helped her sit on the sofa.

Was it all in her head? On top of everything, was she now going crazy?

The spiders appeared from thin air. Spiders that she could not feel. Her throat was still raw from the choking sensation of it closing up again the air. That was real. Holding the towel out, she looked at the crimson stain that splattered and stained the fabric. The blood was real.

"Whoa!" Ezra gasped, looking at her wide-eyed.

Nora looked back to the bathroom. Drips of blood on the sink ran down to the floor, "I know, it sounds insane."

Ezra grabbed the towel and pointed to her, "No, your head!"

Nora lightly touched her head where the blood had oozed from, and it was already feeling sticky to her fingers. The skin felt like it was already sealing itself, "What the...."

"I just watched it seal up! Guess you still have some of the serum in you!" he marveled, leaning in to get a better look.

Nora felt along her forehead, staring at the bloody towel on her lap. There had been more than enough lunacy in the last twenty-four hours, and she decided it must be getting to her. Extreme stress and fatigue did make more sense than phantom spiders.

"I guess I do. I'm sorry if I scared you. I have no idea what that was all about," she said with a small voice, standing on shaky legs to go back to the bathroom to look at the newly formed, red scar on her forehead. A small puddle of blood smeared at her feet. Pulling another towel from the rack, she cleaned it up, still dazed from the shock, "Can you grab some bleach or something? I don't think it's a good idea to have fresh blood calling out to anyone that may be passing by."

Ezra ignored her request, "I'm calling Elijah. We may be a low priority right now, but this is something he should know about."

Nora barely acknowledged his words, wiping the floor repeatedly until the white-tiled bathroom floor shone clean. She took the towel, along with the one she had held to her head, and shuffled mindlessly into her bedroom to place them in her hamper. Sitting on her bed, she snapped back to attention when the misty fog appeared again in the corner of her eye, this time by her door.

"Ezra!" she called out when she turned to find nothing.

He ran into her room, tucking his cell into his pocket, and stopped in the doorway. He sniffed the air and waved a hand in front of his face, "Are you smoking in here?"

"What? No, but I saw that mist again," she crossed the room to the doorway and caught the scent of cigarette smoke, "What the hell is that? What is going on in here?" Nora wanted to run out of the apartment and as far away from Dunhope Manor as possible. The terrors that lay outside seemed to be creeping inside what they had convinced themselves was a safe space. The oddities that were now occurring were adding up and starting to frighten her.

Ezra went to the window to peek at the street below and then quickly walked back to the door, "I called Elijah. He said he's just around the corner doing god knows what, and he said he'd be right over."

Nora stepped out of the bedroom, giving Ezra a little push out as she moved, and closed the door behind them as if she could seal in whatever was happening within the walls. She double and triple-checked the floor to ensure no trace of blood was left. The bloody towels seemed dangerous to have even in the lidded hamper, but she wasn't going to risk entering her room to retrieve them. Staring into the mirror, she found no sign of the spider other than the mark on her head. The fresh scar stayed angrily red, not finishing the healing process as the serum had previously provided. There wasn't much of the fae blood left in her system. Looking at the wide mark, she wondered if it took whatever was left to seal her skin.

Within minutes Elijah, accompanied by two of his fae Glamor Guards, were at the front door. The fae were near matching copies of Greek gods, tall and wide-shouldered with chiseled jaws. The only difference was the golden locks one man had pulled into a tight ponytail at the base of his neck and the other with thick, chocolate curls that sat in a shiny nest atop his head. Nora explained what had happened and started feeling foolish when she heard her words. Elijah sat her down and remained stoic and alert, listening to her description of hallucinated spiders and her lungs tightening shut. The faes' eyes were locked on her until they exchanged a knowing look with Elijah and took to examining the apartment.

"That does sound like quite the fright," Elijah murmured when she finished speaking. He watched the fae move about the room, "The hallucinations could certainly have something to do with the last of the serum leaving your system. I would have thought it would be completely clear of you by now," he turned to Ezra,

"How about you? Have you had any unusual happenings as of late?"

"You're kidding, right?" Ezra guffawed, leveling a look of disbelief at the demon.

"Ezra, you understand what I mean. Anything of the sort that Nora has experienced?"

Ezra thought for a moment, "I'm not seeing spiders or anything. Everything has been a groundhogs day of craziness for me except having my apartment taken away from me this morning."

Elijah pressed his lip in thought, looking at the raw scar that had formed on Nora's face and nodding along to whatever he was thinking. He stood suddenly, moving to Ezra. He took his hand and quickly drew his thumbnail along Ezra's finger. It sliced open as if pierced with a razor blade.

"What the fuck, man? OW!" Ezra snatched his hand back, inspecting the wound, "Why'd you do that?"

Elijah watched the blood pool and then drop from the fresh cut. Ezra fetched a paper towel from the kitchen and wrapped his finger. Nora remained on the couch, watching the bizarre exchange.

"Let me see," Elijah said, holding out his hand.

"No! Don't touch me, psycho!" Ezra fumed, holding his hand away from the demon.

"Don't be foolish, Ezra. Let me see."

Ezra begrudgingly held out his hand, distrust burning in his eyes. Elijah uncovered the wound and found it to be still bleeding. He shared another look with the fae, who stood without any visible emotion.

"A cut that minor would have sealed nearly instantly if there was anything left of the serum from the Ascension left in your bloodstream," Elijah concluded.

"Minor, my ass! That hurt," Ezra grumbled, re-wrapping his fingertip.

The fae moved in unison and took a seat on either side of Nora. They looked her over before the blonde of the set reached for her hand, turning it over. After seeing what Elijah had just done to Ezra, she tried to pull away from a possible slice into her own skin. The fairy was impossibly strong and did not seem to notice her struggling. Instead of pushing a nail into her flesh, he placed his finger on the thin gold line that ran down the center of the ankh branding that another fae had given her. The line began to glimmer, shining against the light for a split second before he released her hand and stood. Giving a quick nod to the second fairy and then to Elijah, the duo of gorgeousness left without a word.

"Oh, dear. Well, that changes things," Elijah said when the door clicked shut.

"What? What changes what?" Nora probed, not understanding the silent exchange of information. Being a mortal among immortals had a way of making anyone feel like an unknowing child.

"The fae blood in the serum was added as a gift from the fae, as you know, and it was supposed to be enough to last for only a fortnight or so," Elijah spoke with his eyes on his phone, awkwardly typing with one finger. It was still amusing to Nora, even in the moment, to watch a demon use a smartphone. It must be something urgent if he was lowering himself to use it. Stealing a quick look, she saw that he was accessing files and not texting. He stepped away when he saw her peeking.

"Why? I mean, why would they want to give it to us?" Ezra asked, his curiosity overcoming his anger toward Elijah.

"Fae blood heals humans, as you well know. If anything were to happen to you while you were being utilized, it was a safety net of sorts. It is also repellant to vampires. It was to keep you safe whilst we used your connections to Jude and Quinn. It also hinders their ability to use their influence on your minds," Elijah answered quickly, bothered by the interruption.

Jude's face came to Nora's thoughts. He had tried to get into her mind and had failed more than once. Now she knew why. That also explained why Gabriel had not wanted even to discuss wiping her memory after 'The Night.' He would not have been able to get around the blood in the serum.

Nora stood to get Elijah's attention, "If it keeps us safe, why is it bad that I still have it in me? Shouldn't we be worried that Ezra doesn't? Get him more if it will keep him safe!"

"It does not work like that, unfortunately. Fae blood is sacred and is not treated as mere contraception against the threat of vampires to humans. As I said, it was a truly generous gift you should be honored to have been given," Elijah scowled at what he read and tucked his cell into his perfectly pressed jacket's inner pocket, "The issue at hand is that a fae cannot be turned. The light inside their blood is countered by the darkness that exists within a vampire's."

Ezra jumped to Nora's side, "So, we can't be turned? That's a good thing. I don't see the problem. Everyone should have a shot of that blood in their system. They wouldn't be able to turn anyone ever again, and we could wipe them all out! A world without vamps sounds pretty good to me," he crowed.

The heat in Elijah's eyes flashed to him before he blinked the reaction away, "Fae are sacred beings and not to be milked like an animal with teats," he seethed, "and either way, that would not help. You see, the fae blood *cannot* be turned. Human blood can. The fight between the light and dark within the weak blood of humans will only have one outcome. Death."

The room stilled with silence as the word reverberated and sunk into their minds. If Jude or Quinn had bitten them, they would have died. Nora wondered if they had known that. Of course, they would have known that. Elijah just told them as if it was common knowledge. What would heal a cut or fractured bone could kill them with a drop of vampire blood. She did not think the risk outweighed the benefits.

"So, if anything happens to Nora, I mean if any of the vamps..." he stopped to look at her, "She'll die?"

"Yes," Elijah replied quietly.

"How is that protecting us? You had us prepped to be killed. I could still be killed," Nora accused, hurt by the realization.

"I guess I'd rather be dead than a vamp," Ezra offered and closed his lips tightly when Nora and Elijah turned agitated stares his way.

"Listen. I told you I would give you more information than I have, and this seems to be a perfect moment to keep that promise. Was there a risk? Yes, of course. However, there were many more benefits than risks. I understand that you feel used. I understand that you feel slighted by the way humans are treated in the grand scheme of things, especially within Aumbry Valley. You must understand that fae are our most sacred beings who make their home on this plane and are the anchor of sorts in the universe's balance. They are not to be used as a product to add comfort and ease to the lives of humans. More importantly, there is only one threat that can cause their demise, and in turn, every one of you who exists here. An ancient, powerful threat born in the deepest bowels of hell. The original vampire's blood. Quinn Goodman now has the maker's pure blood in her possession."

Nora and Ezra stared at Elijah, speechless. Quinn had taken on Jude's fight in the most psychopathic way possible. She was going scorched earth.

"I didn't...I mean, we didn't...know," Ezra whispered.

"Hopefully, now you better understand the battle we are emersed in. I will keep my promise to watch over you, not only because I gave my word to you. It is because I have grown fond of you both. I think I could even go far enough to say you have become friends with me," Elijah spoke slowly, his eyes on the floor in front of him. He gave a slight cough and squared his shoulders, slipping quickly away from the show of emotion, "That being said, I must go."

He moved swiftly to the door, away from the sentimental moment and towards the immortal battle he had to return to. Opening the door, Norman was standing in his doorway, his eyes on Nora's. He stood straight and stiff when Elijah emerged and rushed passed to the stairs.

"Hey, Norman," Nora greeted him softly when she reached the threshold. He looked between her and the distinguished man disappearing down the stairs and closed his door in her face without a word.

Looking down at the scuffed wooden floor of the hallway, Nora saw tiny black bird feathers drifting in the air, and her thoughts turned to Gail. Things kept getting worse and closer to home while poor Norman and Gail were living cluelessly. If anyone was a sitting duck, it was those two. She closed and locked the door before joining Ezra on the sofa.

"Wow," Nora said through an exhale of breath, "That kinda makes our situation seem pretty low on the list, now, doesn't it?"

"Seriously," Ezra said, leaning back against the cushions and raking his uncut hand through his hair, "Your Aunt Quinn is a fucked-up bitch, Nor."

"Yeah, you can say that again," Nora lamented. She touched the sore, fresh scar on her head and hoped it had been enough to clear out the rest of the fae blood. There were already too many ways she was worried that she could die. She did not need one that was a sure thing.

CHAPTER EIGHT

II
B
J
THE HIGH PRIESTESS

The next several days ticked away with very little information being passed onto the two, which they were well accustomed to. They did everything they could to distract themselves from Elijah's revelation, which sounded like the end of days. It was not something that you could tuck away to think about another time, and they were constantly on edge. After they had repeated to each other more than a dozen times that Quinn would absolutely not be able to pull off what they feared she would, they left it at that, agreeing it would not do them any good to discuss the unending possibilities anymore. They pushed the plentiful options from their conversations and tried to settle back into the comfortable routines they created when they were first locked down.

Jenny had been clear that the charms placed on the manor were firmly in place, and they were as secure as they could possibly be as long as the Deficient Duo downstairs stayed out of the way. Their first full day on duty included two of Nora's plates broken, Jack falling down the top flight of stairs when startled by Norman opening his door, and an incorrect report that they had heard of *Lynn's* recapture. After an argument over the super sleuths not even knowing Quinn's name, it was decided they would serve them best by staying downstairs to monitor the front door. Calls to Elijah to replace them had gone unanswered, and when Gabriel asked, he told them it was out of his hands. However, he suggested a way to get rid of them for good. Nora disagreed that eating them would be the most ethical way to relieve them of their post. As long as they stayed out of their hair and could move about the building, they considered it the best they could hope for at the moment. There were bigger fish to fry than Nora and Ezra.

Olivia had been allowed a little more freedom in the building with the decision to have the coven convene in Jenny's apartment. Jenny had been clear that she would rather have everyone gather elsewhere to keep her daughter further away from the intensity of what they were doing. It was for the sake of the spells and their strength to perform them as close to the building as possible that she agreed to the intrusion. With Olivia's promise to stay out of the ballroom that Jenny had relocked and re-hidden the key to, she was allowed to pop in for visits with Nora and Ezra whenever she liked. She usually had at least one meal with them a day, and the slight change in routine had been refreshing. The trio fell into a rhythm that felt as if they were a typical little family, even amid the dangerous chaos, that fact that they weren't a couple and that Olivia wasn't their daughter. Knowing that the little girl was too young to be a part of the coven's work, Jenny was glad to have a happy place for her daughter to play. Ezra and Nora certainly didn't mind. The fresh energy of the little girl was a change of pace in the apartment that had become their shared prison.

Nora could tell that there were things Jenny was keeping from her when she gave glimpses into the work her coven's Elders had been up to, so she was surprised when she was invited to join the group for a discussion of the ongoing plans. Jenny had said it would be best if Ezra or Nora came, and whoever stayed behind could watch Olivia. Nora was sure that Ezra would want to go to get his hands on some information at last and spend some time with Sarah. He insisted that he would be perfectly fine staying with Olivia. The cartoons they preferred would be on during that time anyways, and he once again insisted that Sarah was not his girlfriend. Nora conceded that she must have been wrong about the two and felt terrible for the one-sided feelings that Sarah clearly had. The girl obviously had it bad for him.

Ezra and Nora had debated whether or not she should tell the group what Elijah had revealed to them of Quinn's actions. Nora was sure that they were not the ones that should be passing on information, being mere humans that seemed to be more of a bother than anything at that point, and Ezra thought it was ridiculous to assume that they did not already know. They were witches in a town of supernaturals and had been left to secure the very building that held them—the building with a history directly tied to Jude. If simple humans were in the know, the witches had to have already known. Nora could see that point, even though Jenny had not mentioned any of it to them the few times they had spoken. She wondered if some coven members knew and Jenny did not. That would put Nora in a very tight spot about who could be in the know of what. She quickly missed days of having her head in the sand about what was happening, quieting her curious mind. Ultimately, they decided that she would just listen at the meeting and offer nothing up unless it started from their side. They didn't want to piss off an already overwhelmed demon, even though Elijah had not told them it was confidential information. The paranormal politics were tricky to navigate.

When she left for the meet-up, Ezra and Olivia were curled up on the couch, remote in his hand, and already in deep discussion about one of the characters on the show. Nora smiled at how comfortable they were together and could easily picture him doing the same with his daughter before Jude took away life as he knew it. The bittersweet moment twisted her heart in knots as she walked down to the main floor and an apartment of waiting witches.

The answer to her internal battle of sharing information was over as soon as she walked through the door.

"This does concern all of us! This isn't a fight between the immortals anymore, Eddie!" a woman who appeared to be in her early sixties with frazzled blonde hair she had pulled half up onto her head shouted to a stocky young man with a shaved head and bright, hazel eyes.

"I understand that, Jane. I know the risks. We all know the risks. I'm just saying that we've done enough for these people who will probably skip town as soon as they can. We need to think of the community as a whole," he replied with an even, serious tone.

Jenny gave a terse smile and cleared her throat, "Eddie, let me introduce you to Nora."

Eddie's face washed red with embarrassment, and he stood from his chair, "Oh, I'm...yeah, sorry about that."

Nora waved off the apology and looked at the faces of the strangers who had been helping her for so many weeks. There were thirteen people seated in a circle of mismatched chairs and stools. She was surprised to find an almost equal number of men and women and realized that her fairy tale idea of witches had her assuming they would all be female. It's not like they would be a group of old hags in pointed hats and riding brooms. She had known Jenny long enough to know that witches were just like anyone else, apart from the magical skills they seemed to possess. The group looked back at her from the circle that included the plump, pink floral armchair which Olivia preferred. Instead of the tiny little girl, the chair held a distinguished-looking woman whose shimmering honey eyes were set on Nora. Her long hair, black as night and swirled with tiny silvery streaks, was slung over her shoulder in a braid that reached her lap. A large blue crystal that appeared to glow from within was set in silver and strung on an intricate chain around her neck. Her bright eyes bore into Nora's as if she could see past them and directly into her mind and soul.

"Priestess, may I introduce Nora Goodman? Nora, this our High Priestess, Priestess Maren," Jenny introduced. Her voice was quiet and full of reverence for the impressive woman.

"It's lovely to finally meet you, Miss Goodman," she replied, remaining in her seat. Nora noticed a wooden cane propped up against the side of the chair.

Stepping toward the circled group, she smiled at each person before she spoke to High Priestess Maren, "It's an honor to meet you, ma'am. I want to take the opportunity to thank you, to thank all of you for helping us. Ezra is thankful, as well. We're so grateful for your generosity."

"A friend of Jenny's is a friend of our coven, dear," she offered kindly and pointed to a couple of empty chairs across from her that Jenny and Nora moved to sit in, "I am aware that our friend Elijah Beasley has told you of what your family has been up to. That we now know that Quinn possesses the powerful blood of the Maker."

The group murmured to each other angrily at the mention. Nora nodded, glad that she would not have to keep that information for herself. The way Maren looked at her made her think that there wasn't anything that she could keep from her, spoken or otherwise. An ethereal energy radiated from her, both welcoming and intimidating at once.

"I just can't wrap my head around how a baby vampire could cause so much havoc and do all that she has in such a short amount of time. Jude, I get it, but this lady?

How?" a slight and nervous-looking woman interjected. She tugged at her soft brown curls as she spoke, shaking her head.

"Because of Jude, Rosa!" two voices spoke the words at once. The man, pale with thin champagne hair clipped close, and a wide-eyed woman with hair as blue as her eyes, "Obviously."

"Nora, this is Briella and Brian, our resident twin witches," Jenny volunteered.

"And resident pain in the asses," another woman, eyes as dark as the deep chocolate waves that tumbled along her tense and grumpy face down to her thin but stiff shoulders.

"Shut up, Frida," the twins sneered.

Jenny laughed at the exchange, "Yeah, so that's Frida," Jenny repeated, and the woman gave Nora a nod, "and we also have Jackson," she pointed to a young man with a broad smile and ashy-blonde hair he tucked behind his ears. Jenny continued along the circle, "Jimmy," a wide-chested man with closely set eyes and a friendly smirk, "Oliver," an older man with soft white hair smoothed slick to his head and a mischievous grin, "You already know Sarah, and this is Ryder, or Red-Ryder as we call him."

Ryder had deep auburn hair that tumbled down his back in shining curls and a thick, well-manicured beard to match. Nora gave each of them another friendly smile and sat awkwardly, not knowing what to say after saying hello.

Luckily, Maren broke the silence, "They have all been hard at work dealing with the newest dilemma The Firm has been tasked with, and I am very proud of all of them," she gave them the proud smile of a mama bear.

"No disrespect to you, Priestess, but it's not The Firm; it's the bureau. B.I.T.N. is always the one causing drama," Frida growled, "The Firm needs to shut them down."

"We shouldn't be so involved in any of their shit, anyways," Eddie muttered, "What have they ever done for us?"

"We have been over this. The balance of the valley is a balance that affects us all. We do not do good for the sake of reward. We do good for the sake of good," Maren said firmly, "and we will not be discussing it again."

"And we have to acknowledge that Quinn and her fellow nutters are going after the fae. The fae! That makes all of this bigger than just vampires fighting for power amongst themselves. The fae would never allow their kind to be wiped out! Which you all know would wipe us all out in turn, or at the very least, the source of our powers, and you know it! But if they feel threatened, you know they will bring in the big guns. That's not a battle; that's war!" Jane blurted out quickly.

The big guns? Nora didn't like the sounds of something more potent than the fae and desperately wanted to know what that meant. Her mind was thumping with questions, and she bit the inside of her cheek to keep herself silent. The witches seemed more open to discussing issues in front of plain-old humans than other supernatural beings, and Nora wanted to absorb as much as possible.

"I agree with Eddie," Sarah said quietly, her eyes on the ground in front of her, "I think keeping the charms up on this place is all we owe anyone or anything. There's no need for us to entwine ourselves further in this."

"This will blow over in a few days like everything else around here. Will some of them get hurt or worse? Of course. They always do. Do we need to risk ourselves? Hell no," Eddie contested, "I say we keep our heads down, keep out of it as much as we can and let them handle their own mess for once."

Nora's head spun from witch to witch as they debated how far they should get themselves involved. They knew the risk of what could happen if Quinn was successful in her attack on the fae, and they related it to other battles that had taken place in the past. Some that they had been involved in, some that their ancestors had. The valley's history was rife with conflicts, and the witches had been involved by choice or attack for centuries. Nora felt even more thankful for their help when it became clear that the witches were not mortals that tinkered with spells and potions; they were warriors with war in their blood. At the end of the conversation, it was concluded that they also did not think there was a strong probability Quinn would be able to pull it off. Nora was hoping with all of her might that they were right.

By the time they stood and broke off into informal chats, Nora had learned some of their ways and where they stood on the issue. She was disappointed that they did not provide further information on Quinn's movement or what was to come. They did not seem to know much more than she already did in that department. It did give her faith in Elijah that he was giving her all the information he could if she was up to speed in the same way as the coven. In the end, it left her feeling that there was no way she could contribute in any way other than to sit tight and wait.

It was becoming her unwanted slogan.

She thanked each one for their help and repeatedly apologized for her aunt and the bother they all had brought upon Aumbry Valley. Priestess Maren gently took her elbow and slowly guided her towards the door with heavy weight on her cane, stopping just before they reached the exit.

"You're a trusting soul, aren't you, Nora Goodman? Feisty, but trusting," she posed the query, yet seemed to know the answer.

"I guess I am. I feel like I can trust you guys, that's for sure," Nora replied with a slight, grateful grin.

"I'm glad to hear that, dear," she said, her eyes scanning the ceiling, seeing and hearing things beyond Nora's senses, "You should know that blind trust always leads to darkness. A pure heart like your own is a gift and curse all at once," Nora's heart picked up pace when the Priestess' serious gaze locked in on her, "There are many energies that exist within these walls. Just as many secrets, I can see. What I ask of you is that you consider who you trust and who you think you know. Strong powers are at work under this roof, and not all of it is ours."

"I'm not sure what you mean by that," Nora said quietly, "There are threats here? In Dunhope?"

"Oh, honey, there are threats in every inch of the universe. Not everything we need to watch for is threats. That would drive the strongest mind mad," she chuckled deeply at the idea, "What I am saying is that you are new to what you see under the veil. When everything seems strange, it all blurs together. Nothing in this valley is black or white, right or wrong. Once you're under the veil, you need to look deeper. You have to see the layers. Do you understand?"

"I'm not sure. I guess I do," Nora replied, trying to sort out what she had been told. It did seem foolish to give blanket trust to anyone in a world that she knew little of.

Priestess Maren released Nora's elbow and reached into a velvet satchel strung on her wrist. She pulled out a worn stack of cards, holding them out on her flat palm, "Touch the tarot, dear."

Nora nervously reached her hand towards them and set her hand on top. Priestess Maren closed her eyes, a half smile ticking up on her lips when she nodded whatever she was receiving, "Cut the deck for me."

Nora picked up the top third of the cards and held it over the others, "Like this?"

"Yes, dear. Now turn it over."

Nora complied. The card revealed *Temperance* written in scratchy ink under a worn-looking illustration, "Is that good?"

"It's neither good nor bad, Nora. It simply is," Maren smiled at the confusion on Nora's face, "What do you see?"

"The word Temperance."

She kept a steady gaze on Nora, watching her with interest, "Yes, and?"

Nora described the wide-winged angel illustrated above the word and the two golden cups in their hand.

"Good. What else?"

Nora didn't know what else to say. That was all that she saw that was pictured.

"Look at their feet. What do you see?" Maren pushed.

Looking at the feet, she saw one was in the water, and one was on land. She asked if that was what she meant, and Maren gave her the proud smile she had witnessed her give to the coven, "But what does that mean?"

"One foot in one world, one in another, honey. Just like you," the High Priestess declared. She took the cards from Nora and placed the deck back in her satchel but kept the card they were discussing in hand, "Testing the waters and being aware," she handed the card to Nora, taking the stunned girl's free hand and placing it on top, "Seeing the little things within the card, just like you need to see the little things that make up your new world. Quinn is a threat. The new world exists around that. It's what else you can see that makes up the whole picture. What makes up life," she looked Nora over in silence for a moment before continuing her puzzling advice, "Keep that card with you. Take in all of the little details that make it up and what they could mean. It will remind you that what you see on the surface isn't all there is to look for." With that, she walked away without another word, gesturing for her fellow members of the coven to rejoin the circle. They silently stood in front of the chairs they had previously occupied.

'I'll be up soon,' Jenny mouthed to Nora with a nod, letting her know it was time to go.

Nora stood for a beat with questions burning to be asked. Clearly, she was being dismissed, and it seemed disrespectful to overstay her welcome with the ones choosing to be on her side of the newest insanity Quinn had brought down on her. She stared at the card that had been pressed into her hand when she made her way to the hallway and up the stairs.

The Priestess' warning spun in her thoughts like a fever dream when she took each step up the three flights to her apartment. The fact that there were people she shouldn't trust did seem like common sense when dealing with demons and vampires, let alone the secretive fae. It was what she said about energies in the building. She hoped those energies were nothing more than something drifting about like memories and could not touch her. The little things that she had to look under the surface for. The tiny spiders she saw in the mirror skittered their legs into her mind, worrying her that it was more than just the serum leaving her system. The little things could mean a death of a thousand paper cuts. Or spider bites.

CHAPTER NINE

ACE of SWORDS.

Ezra and Olivia were still sitting in the same spots on the sofa when she returned. Nora could not look away from the tarot card in her hand when she sat beside them, not noticing Ezra staring expectantly at her for the details of the meeting. Silas slunk off Ezra's lap and onto hers, bringing her attention back into the room.

"Well?" he asked, sitting up straighter in his seat.

"They already knew," she looked to Olivia, who was still enthralled in the cartoon, "about what Elijah said."

"They knew? And Je...," he leaned towards Nora, lowering his voice, "*she* didn't tell us?"

Nora pressed her lips at the thought. Jenny did not owe them anything, let alone to give out information that they may have been told to keep to themselves. Ezra and Nora were unsure if they should speak of it, so it seemed fair that Jenny did the same. The way they spoke freely in front of her was enough to know that they trusted her. They didn't pause to explain what they were debating, even Jenny, so there was an unspoken understanding that Nora realized at that moment, "They knew we knew, so I guess she didn't think we needed to talk about it."

"So, what all did they say?" Ezra pushed, leaning further over the arm of the couch as if that was enough to keep the exchange from Olivia's little ears.

Nora nodded towards the kitchen, and they moved to the counter, adding another twenty feet of privacy. The little girl stayed focused on the TV and the box of cheesy crackers beside her.

"Not a lot more than Elijah said the other day. I mean, that's pretty well all they discussed," Nora shared, her voice low, "There was a lot of back and forth about whether they should be involved at all. I wasn't expecting a cauldron and little jars of bones or anything, but it was really rather mundane. It was more like a city council meeting than a gathering of witches. Although they were discussing life and death matters. That's a little bigger than where to put a new stop sign."

"Did they say anything about what they're planning on doing? Do they know what's going on with the BITN crews? They've been sent off somewhere on something big. I know it," Ezra said with a frown. Nora was getting worried about how much he had been thinking about joining the crews in the past few days. Not that she wanted him to leave with her as much as she worried that his hatred of vampires was starting to take over his mind. If he couldn't focus on anything else, he would never be able to find closure with his past. The concern crossed her mind at least once a day, but she had yet to find the courage to speak up. As close as they had become, he was still someone she hadn't even known for a year. Telling him how to live his life felt intrusive. Even though she knew she was right.

"I'm not sure why they invited me to join them," Nora said instead, "I just sat and listened. Even still, it was nice to be able to meet them and thank them."

"Did they say they had any idea where Quinn was?"

"Not much that they said. They mostly went back and forth about how much they should be involved," Nora gave the card a once over and set it on the counter in front of her.

Ezra picked it up and turned it over curiously, "What's this?"

"Their High Priestess, Maren, gave it to me. She was interesting, to say the least."

"What's the purpose of this thing? Is it magic like your rock?" Ezra needled.

Nora snatched back the card and set it on the opposite counter, out of his reach, "She was going on about who to trust and seeing the big picture. That there were powers in the building that we didn't know about or understand. I don't know. It was all very cryptic. She said this card would help me with clarity or something."

"So, magic rocks and fortune-telling cards? That's their big plan to get us all through this? Awesome," Ezra griped and slumped against the kitchen island.

"They're doing whatever they can, and we should be grateful, Ezra. One guy didn't seem to want anything to do with any of it. He was clear on that point."

"That's Eddie," Olivia's voice chimed in. They found her head popped up over the couch; cheesy cracker dust spread across her lips. She licked some more from her fingers, "Eddie hates vampires almost as much as you, Ezra."

Nora hadn't considered what all Olivia knew of the supernatural goings on all around her. Jenny had been clear that she did not want her daughter around when the coven was gathering. Nora had not considered that this could be due to the current situation and that she would usually be more aware of the witches and their goings-on. The little girl was keenly aware of the world around her, too smart for her own good at times. It was foolish to think she was oblivious to everything that happened within the valley and Dunhope Manor.

"What do you know about vampires, Olivia?" Ezra asked, his voice light as if he was just playing around with her. His eyes were more serious than his tone.

"What don't I know, silly? My mom's a witch. I kinda know a lot about a lot," she grinned and bounced on the couch, her little cheesy fingers holding on to the back cushion.

A knock on the door announced Jenny's arrival as if on cue. Nora gave Olivia a curious look and opened the locks. She would have liked to have had a chance to pry further into what she knew.

"Hey, thanks for watching her, Ez. I appreciate it. I hope she was good?" Jenny inquired with her eyes on the smiling little mop top still standing on the couch.

"She was a perfect angel," Ezra replied, "As usual."

Olivia gave him a proud smile and jumped down from the couch. She spooked Silas from the chair he had curled up in, and he gave her a bothered yowl when she skipped passed him to join the other three, wiping her cheesy fingers on her shirt, "I'm not an angel, dummy. I'm just a person."

"Oh, my apologies, she was a perfect person," Ezra laughed, "She was just telling us about Eddie and how he hates *vampires*."

"Olivia, what did I tell you about talking about people that aren't in the room?" Jenny chided. She grabbed a tea towel from the rack to rub at the girl's messing hands and face.

"I know, mommy, but they were talking about him first," she whined, "So, they should be in trouble too."

"So, she knows about vampires and…all the rest?" Nora asked with surprised curiosity. The time they spent with her felt like she was just a regular little girl in a regular little town. They should have known better knowing what they knew of Aumbry Valley.

"She's born and raised here, descended from generations of witches. She was bound to start realizing what was going on all around her at some point," Jenny said plainly and picked the girl up to set her on her hip, "I don't want to raise her with secrets that I don't have to have. It's going to be her future after all. Wouldn't you have liked to be more eased into this insanity?" she asked with a laugh. Ezra and Nora replied with raised brows and nods.

Jenny thanked them again and said she would be up to talk about the coven meeting later. Olivia shuffled her legs about, asking to be let down. As soon as her sneakers hit the ground, she ran to Norman's door and gave a series of quick knocks. A response of a similar knock came from the other side of the door. Whatever the meaning was, it made Olivia giggle, and she took off for the stairs singing one of her made-up songs. This one featured herself flying in the clouds with the sun on her face, and her cheery little voice disappeared down the stairs.

"It may be tomorrow that I come up if this one doesn't chill out," she leveled her eyes on Ezra, her jaw set with judgment.

"Hey! This one isn't on me. I didn't give her any candy at all this time! Just the cheese crackers!" Ezra said, his hands up in innocence.

Jenny just shook her head with a laugh and took off after her little ball of energy, giving a wave over her shoulder.

Back in the apartment and settled on the couch, Nora held the tarot card and shared more of what the Priestess had said.

"What the hell is any of that supposed to mean? There's energy and secrets in the walls? That could mean anything," Ezra said after turning over the words more than once in his head. He took the card and stared at it as if the answers would reveal themselves.

"Especially in this town and this place," Nora agreed, looking around them in search of any hint of what the woman had meant, "What worries me most is that she said to watch who we trust. That could be anyone. How does that help? Should we stop trusting everyone?"

It felt hopeless to think what that would be like as a future if they remained in that town. She admitted to herself that, knowing what they knew now, if they ever did leave the valley, they wouldn't be able to trust anyone ever again unless they were able to have their memories erased. Which would leave them with a blind side that could be even more dangerous than the average mortal walking through life. They were on the radar of powerful supernatural beings that were well aware of them, whether Nora and Ezra knew or not. Nora held her head at the flood of possibilities she had been blissfully ignoring for the past few days. Guilt washed over her when the idea of getting rid of Quinn presented itself as a quick stop to her problems. Not that she was the only threat out there, anyways. With Quinn gone, there was still a risk of others who could still blindly see her as a leader or even want to retaliate for Jude's demise.

"I think you know me well enough to know there are very few people in the world that I trust. It's a pretty short list: myself, my sister, probably Olivia," he gave half of a laugh at that fact, "and you."

Nora looked up from her suffocating spiral of thoughts when he spoke, "You really trust me?"

"You have to know that I do," he said softly, "I didn't think there was anyone I could trust again, outside of my family. Anyone that I could," he paused, and Nora wasn't sure if he wanted to finish his thought until he did, "that

I could open up to. You know, someone that could make me smile again."

She was glad that he could trust her. She knew that she felt the same way about him. They had literally saved each other's lives from vampire attacks, and shared near-death experiences tend to breed trust. It at least grew a profound bond within them. He smiled and picked up Silas, "We have this guy that we can trust as long as we don't have food he wants," she laughed when he hopped back off her lap and strolled to the kitchen, "Sarah and her cooking make you smile, too," Nora giggled.

"Aaaaagh!" he bellowed, "Stop with that, will you? She's not my girlfriend. She's not going to be my girlfriend. End of story. The end, okay?"

Nora grimaced at his outburst. She could see that she had teased him one time too many, "Sorry. I was just trying to be funny."

Ezra frowned in return to Nora's downturned lips, "Sorry. It's just...anyways. I just wanted to say that I'm glad we met. You and me. It's the one good thing in this mess."

Nora was relieved that his mood did not turn dark as it used to when he would get upset. The past few months had lightened the load that he carried on his shoulders. Redirecting his emotions into hatred of vampires had that one positive effect. Nora admitted for the first time that she might also have something to do with his change in attitude. They had become very good friends, close as family in a way, and that would make him as close to a best friend as she'd had since Quinn had left her. He was right. At the end of the day, and hopefully, at the end of their time in Dunhope Manor, something good came of it all.

"You do make a good roommate. Even though your cooking sucks," she said with a dramatic shudder.

"Maybe I'm an excellent chef, and I'm just tricking you into doing all the work," he retorted, giving her leg a playful slap.

"I'll give you that you make a passable breakfast if you stay away from the bacon," she conceded.

"Thank you. I think my toast is quite good," he said with a grin, "And, hey, I think we're more than roommates, don't you?"

Nora turned to him, unsure how to respond or what exactly he was implying, "How do you mean?"

"Well, I'd say we're cellmates," and laughed, "and *cellies* are for life."

The alarm on the kitchen counter rang out and reverberated against every surface of the apartment. They jumped from the couch with fright-filled yelps. Looking to the windows, they found the sun setting quickly; a deep purple haze on the horizon was all that was left.

"Looks like the day got away from us," Nora said, moving to start their routine of securing windows and blinds. Ezra headed into the bedroom, and Nora took the living room.

"AHHH!" Ezra's scream howled out into the apartment, "Motherfucker!"

Nora dashed to find Gabriel floating happily on the other side of her bedroom window, humor twitching at his lips as he watched Ezra's surprise.

"What are you doing? Damn it, Gabriel," she scolded and tugged up the window before stepping back quickly. It wasn't distrust of Gabriel that had her keeping her distance. It was whatever else could be out there with him. At least, she hoped that's what it was and not a new fear of Gabriel, her only friend outside of the building. Priestess Maren had sown the seeds of distrust that bloomed in her every thought now.

"Calm down, Nervous Nelly! I swear. You two get more dramatic every time I see you!" he propped his chin up on his fist as he casually leaned an elbow on the windowsill.

"Speaking of those I don't trust," Ezra growled, his jovial mood evaporating with the arrival of the playful vampire, "What do you want, Gabriel?"

"Easy, handsome. You know I'm one of the good guys," he purred.

"Yeah, sure," Ezra sniffed and started to leave.

"Ezra, seriously! You're being childish. You know Gabriel would never do anything to hurt us. Hell, how many times can I point out that he saved our lives? You can't just forget about that," Nora snapped, "This fighting has to stop."

"Yeah, don't be like that. You know you love me, somewhere down in that big 'ol heart," Gabriel drawled in a poor cowboy accent, "I'm better protection than Tweedle-dee and Tweedle-dumb that they have stationed downstairs. One of which is sleeping on the couch, I'll have you know, and the other one is not even in the building. I'd be insulted if I were you," he sneered, "Either way, forget those botched blood bags. I come with hot gossip that might interest you."

Ezra stopped in his tracks and turned, although not taking a step back toward him, "Do you know what's going on? Where's Quinn? Why isn't Elijah answering our calls anymore?"

Gabriel held up a hand to silence the onslaught of questions, "That man isn't answering mine either, so don't take that personally. Whatever they're up to is above my purview, and my pay grade. I guess the risk of the end of times doesn't need my assistance," Gabriel said, picking at a troublesome cuticle on his thumb.

"You seem pretty casual about something that seems pretty damn serious," Nora said, exasperated, "Everyone is being so up and down with this. Is it bad or just another supernatural battle that you all seem to live in *every frigging day?*"

"Oh, of course, it's a dangerous situation, Nora, my sweet little blood peach. But you can't live as long as I have, and through all that, I have without learning that the joy in life is in the fun and laughter. I'm already technically dead, and you both started dying the moment you were born. Depressing, right? There are barely any new shows worth a binge—a travesty. Oh, and let's not forget that climate change thing they're always banging on about. I may live long enough to see that happen, you know. They need to think of the vampires, dammit! Can't you see that life is merely death and suffering without someone like me to make it lighter? I'm a damn universal treasure."

Nora and Ezra stared back, slack-jawed, at the irreverent vampire.

"You are truly insane," Ezra finally said.

"That very well could be, but you're going to want to hear what I have to say, fella," Gabriel winked and leaned closer to the window, "Nora's little dream boat Rowan and all the rest of them have been given the Ascension. They are full up to their nipples with fae serum," he said with the smile of a cat who swallowed a canary and twinkle in his eye. This vampire adored gossip.

"Bully for them. Why should we care?" Ezra said, losing interest quickly. His voice was heavy with jealousy.

"Ezra, you, of all people, should care because they're amping up the crews within B.I.T.N., especially after they saw the lackluster recruits that they rustled up for you two," Gabriel jeered.

"So, are they coming back now? Rowan, Melissa, and the crew?" Nora asked, hoping for more security back and the normality and friendships they had started to form.

"Oh, no. They're moving up in the world. They won't be given little assignments like you two."

"Then what does any of this have to do with us?" Ezra asked, his patience thin.

"Well..." Gabriel stopped to give a theatrical pause, his eyes twinkling, "that has everything to do with you because I've heard word that you are recruit *numero uno* that they are looking at for a new squad," he raised an eyebrow, excitedly waiting for Ezra's response.

"Wait, what? Are you serious?" he asked excitedly and moved swiftly to the open window.

"I am. They'll probably approach you tomorrow," Gabriel shared, happy with Ezra's reaction, "You have to act surprised, though. I mean it. I don't want to get a reputation as a gossip."

Nora snorted a laugh before turning to Ezra, "Come on, you would consider joining them? Like really joining them? Not like how we have been. That wouldn't be on the sidelines anymore. Ez. That would be truly dangerous. Constantly dangerous."

"You both already have the brand, so technically, you've already joined us. He's just going to be given something to do. A chance to get out of this decrepit building," he looked beyond them into the apartment with a sore expression.

"And a chance to take out some vamps!" Ezra exclaimed, excitement racing across his eyes.

"Easy there, killer. No need to be rude," Gabriel sneered, "You should know there is a catch."

"What?" Ezra asked with expectant disappointment dripping in his tone.

"There is a lot of redirection of how things are being done now. You know, with all of the royal fuck ups that have been happening. They've changed how they hire mortals now. A sort of insurance. It's a lifetime post, now, Ezra," Gabriel announced flatly.

"What? That's crazy. You can't commit to something like that!" Nora exclaimed. There was no way he would pledge the rest of his life to work among the very beings he was quite clear in despising.

"The hell I can't!" Ezra cheered, happiness pushing a massive grin across his face. He could not stand still as the possibilities raced in his mind.

He had been tossing up the idea of doing something to help until they could move on from the nightmare of a town that held them. That was one side of a very different coin. Now he was willing to dedicate his life, his entire life, to staying in Aumbry Valley and putting his life on the line for the chance to take the life of a vampire. She couldn't believe there was so much hate for vampires inside of him that he would live his life specifically for a chance to hurt them. She knew he didn't hate Gabriel, especially in the way that he did Jude. That was mostly an act. She knew in her heart that he could not still be so angry at the world that he would set himself up to self-destruct. Going into it with that mindset was a deadly combination that Nora worried Elijah was not taking into account. She worried that she had not taken his words about vampires as more than simple venting. He had just seemed so positive. So hopeful. Looking at Ezra's giddy expression, she realized she did not know that to be true after all. He would gladly give the rest of his life to the Bureau and The Firm as a whole. She had no idea what would come of her future, but now she was more concerned for Ezra's.

"Ugh, here comes Tweedle-dumb down the street. I'm out of here. Talking with him is too mentally painful," Gabriel leered down at the bumbling man they had been gifted with before disappearing in a blink into the night sky. Nora stared out at the space where he had been floating as she slid the window shut and latched the lock. Once again, their lives were about to change completely.

CHAPTER TEN

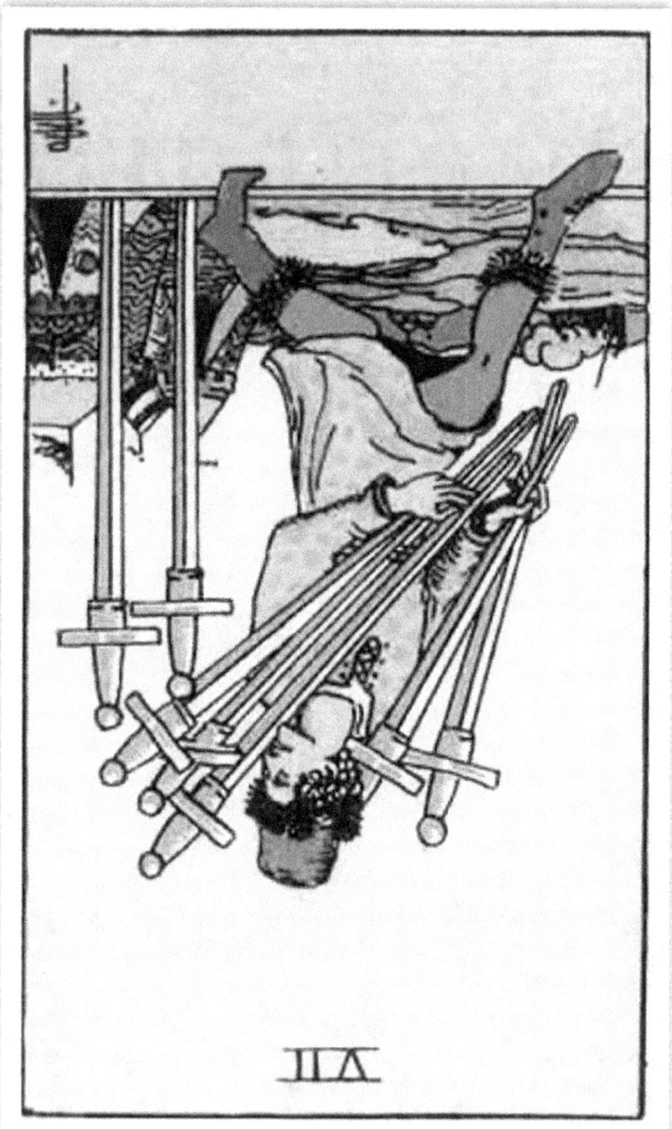

The next day, Jenny came up with Olivia in tow and went directly to the coffee. The deep rings that sat swollen beneath her eyes told Nora that Ezra may not have been entirely truthful when he said he hadn't given Olivia any sweet treats the day before. Even Olivia was moving slowly, dragging her feet with tow-headed hair thrown into a half attempt at a ponytail. She tightly hung on to the ballerina doll they had brought down from the ballroom.

"Did you hear the news?" Ezra, well-rested and full of energy, asked excitedly as soon as they crossed the threshold.

Jenny blinked deeply at his volume, "If you're talking about your impending recruitment to a crew, it seems it's old news. Jack and Belinda just bitched and moaned for the last ten minutes to me about it," Jenny said through a long yawn, "I kind of regret letting them set up shop there."

"What did they have to bitch about?" Nora asked. To begin with, the two were found to be unlikeable in the short passings she had with them. They would be wise not to snipe about anyone and risk making real enemies of them.

"I don't know. They're pissed that they were up for a new assignment, and then he got it, and blah, blah, blah. It was all whiny bitching to me. They obviously can not tell when someone does not care what they're talking about," Jenny rolled her eyes above the coffee mug.

"They've been here, like, a week, and they're complaining? They may as well leave, anyways. Not like they're effective," Nora asserted. It had been days since Quinn's escape, and they had not heard hide or hair of her. Even if she were to appear, it would not be difficult to get by the bumbling duo. If anything, they would be more likely to accidentally stake one of them or burn down the place trying to figure out a microwave.

"Exactly. I don't even know why they're still here. Waste of space if you ask me," Ezra said, still beaming, "I gotta go to my place. There's something I have to find." His grin was splitting his face when he gave Olivia's loose curl a good-natured tug before heading downstairs.

"What a dork," Jenny remarked, "It's nice to see him excited about something again, though. I was worried his skin was going to start merging with your couch and remote."

"I wonder if he'll stay in the building when he starts with them?" Nora wondered aloud, "I just realized I have no idea where the rest of the crew lives. Do you think they have houses or a big dormitory or something?" As much as she considered them friends, it occurred to her that she knew very little about them. It would be pretty lonely if Ezra had to move into a barracks-type situation.

"I doubt he'll leave this apartment unless he has to," Jenny quipped, re-filling her coffee mug, "He's pretty comfy right where he is."

"He said this is his favorite place in the whole world," Olivia piped up from the couch. She was struggling to get the TV on and slapped the remote on her palm.

"I highly doubt that Aumbry Valley is his favorite place, cutie-pie," Nora laughed, "He probably meant being on the couch with you. You guys do have a lot of fun, huh?"

"No, Norma, he said here," Olivia asserted, waving her hand around at the apartment, "Up here in this apartment."

Nora dipped her head to hide the flush that spoke more of her feelings than her mind or lips would allow. It seems the teasing of a *Nezra* coupling, as Jenny had named them, had spread to the little one, as well. She opened a juice box, slipped in the straw, and put it in Olivia's hands, hoping to silence her. She took the remote and turned the channel to one of her cartoons for good measure.

"So, anyways," Nora said to Jenny, quickly changing the subject, "Is it okay to talk about yesterday? What happened with your coven? I mean, can we talk about it with her here?"

Jenny nodded in her daughter's direction, "Yeah, sure. There's little she doesn't know about."

"Okay. The High Priestess, Maren?" Nora asked as Jenny got comfortable on a kitchen stool, "She said something strange about energies in the building and not trusting everyone. What was she talking about?"

"The trust advice is just plain good advice, so it may only mean that. With all of the moles in The Firm right now, it's hard to know who is on whose side. As to how she probably said it, Priestess Maren likes to spin word puzzles of a sort that are supposed to help us become more in tune with our own minds and spirits. Sometimes it makes sense right away, sometimes it takes a while, and sometimes it just seems like nonsense," Jenny laughed, "I can tell you what I know about the energies she talks about. Not what it is, I have no idea what it is, but she says this building holds powerful energy that needs to be protected. She made a huge scene about it when I wanted to sell after we lost Mark. It's been something she's been trying to get me to practice more. Sensing spirits and energies and the like," Jenny shook her head, wistfully staring into her steaming mug, "I'm just not that strong of a witch, I guess."

Nora hated seeing her friend doubt herself, "Don't say that! You're incredible. You're keeping us safe, aren't you?"

"The coven is. I'm just helping," Jenny grumbled.

Nora remembered the previous conversation with Sarah and Ezra, "Sarah said you're like the second in command of the coven. How is that possible if you aren't good at what you do?"

"That's all family politics and nothing to do with my skills," Jenny sighed and watched her daughter for a moment, "I left the craft well before I met Mark, and then we both got pulled back in. I thought it would just be a temporary thing until we could leave and then Mark...well, then it was just us," she said quietly, looking at Olivia happily watching her shows, "Before I knew what was happening, she started to show signs of abilities about a year ago. Very unusual at that age. Rare even, and just like that, we had to stay. She needs to be among a coven. It's the safest place for her."

"What do you mean, abilities?" Nora asked, shocked that she didn't know the sweet little girl who practically lived on her couch was growing up to be a powerful witch. She had never noticed anything unusual about her other than she seemed mature for her age.

"It started with her sensing moods—more than just reading faces or tones. You could be sitting there, stone-faced, and she would know what was going on in your mind," Jenny explained, her voice low.

"Like...she can read our minds?" Nora whispered as well as if a quiet voice would matter to a telepathic child.

Jenny shook her head, "No, not like that. She can't read thoughts or anything. She just knows how you're feeling, even when you might not even realize it yet."

"That's crazy," Nora said with awe. She knew Olivia was a special little girl. She hadn't considered her to be supernaturally special as well.

"Yeah. That was crazy enough. Then one day, she was having a fit about wanting waffles instead of cereal," Jenny started.

"I hate cereal!" Olivia shouted from her seat without turning around.

"I know, baby," Jenny answered with a tired laugh, "Anyways, I put down the cereal, turned to get her some juice, and when I turned back, the milk had curdled. I checked the carton, and the milk was fine. I poured her another bowl, poured the fresh milk, and watched as she curdled it again. Right in front of my eyes."

"And I don't have to have cereal anymore, Norma!" Olivia cheered. She was standing on the couch, raising her doll over her head in victory.

Nora stared back at the girl who looked so normal, "I'm glad I never gave you any then! That would have scared the pants off of me," she stammered.

Olivia laughed, "Don't be silly, Norma. Magic isn't something to be scared of."

"Easy for her to say," Nora mumbled to Jenny. Every day, Aumbry Valley revealed more of its secrets and became more frightening each time. Nora wondered how long it would take for all of it to start feeling normalized.

Olivia laughed at Nora's unease and started to jump on the couch cushions. She stopped with one swift glare from her mother.

"This place is just too much," Nora marveled, "I guess there are a lot of reasons people stay in Aumbry Valley, huh?"

"More than I can count. This place tends to get its hooks into you, and it never let's go," Jenny said, making Nora growl with frustration. She saw the truth in that statement more and more with each passing day. Even

Quinn Goodman, *woman of the world*, could not shake her ties to that town.

"I'm pretty sure I want to leave. When I can, I mean. I don't know. As awful as everything has been, you all have become like family to me. I don't know if I could leave you all," she looked over her apartment, "Although, no offense to you and Dunhope Manor, but I've spent enough time inside these walls that I'd at least like to leave *this* place," Nora half-heartedly chuckled.

Jenny smiled and raised her mug in agreement, "Listen, there's no reason for you to stay locked up in this cage. The locks on that door aren't doing as much as the charms on the building are. If Quinn wanted in, she'd find a way in. The sun is stopping that right now. Any familiar she may have working for her won't be able to get in the building at all, with it all locked up," she stood to rinse her mug, "Come downstairs for breakfast with us. The change of scenery will do you good," Jenny offered, rubbing her hand lovingly on her back.

Nora liked the idea of something, anything, new that wasn't a new fright. She couldn't help but think that the status quo had kept them safe so far and breaking the rules might not be the best move, "I don't know, we're supposed to...."

Jenny interrupted, "Who cares what you're supposed to do?" "Who's going to stop you? Nothing happened when you came down yesterday."

Nora thought for a moment, "That was different, though, wasn't it?" Nora stopped when Jenny posed her mommy glare to her, "I guess the two Moron Minions downstairs aren't saying anything about Ezra leaving here, are they?"

She had become so used to sitting in her apartment and waiting for news or direction that it had made her frightened to do anything else. It was more nerve-racking to think of having a friendly visit downstairs than the constant threat of possible vampire retribution. The realization was instantly freeing to Nora. She was creating a jail within her prison that did not need to exist. She was talking about leaving the valley eventually and would have to start living her life. That may as well start with breakfast with Jenny. Rowan's words whispered in her thoughts.

Gotta get wet sometimes, Nora.

Jenny seemed to notice the red streak across Nora's cheeks with the thought but only smiled, "Exactly, and my place has just as many charms. Just not as many locks," Jenny said, pointing her thumb at the stack of locks on the door, "and better still, I have mimosas!"

Nora laughed and nodded to that selling point, "Okay, let's do it."

Olivia jumped up from the couch, clapping, "Yay! A breakfast party!"

"No cereal, though, right?" Nora teased and switched off her television.

"No way!" Olivia giggled. The sweet sound had Nora feeling even more at ease as they walked out the door.

When they made it to the second floor, Nora told the two that she would let Ezra know what they were doing so he could join them. When Olivia excitedly pulled at her mother's hand, Jenny said she would meet them downstairs.

Walking down the hall to his apartment, Nora laughed at the feathers dusting the floor from Gail's apartment. Ezra was right; it was a mess down there. The singing of the birds, especially one very out-of-tune avian, filled the echoing hallway around her. It was strange that the sound never made its way up or down to the other floors. Spending even a minute there made her glad for the thickly-built walls of old buildings. Passing Gail's door, she noticed it was open a crack. A beautiful white feather drifted out with the warbles of the birds. Having an open door made Nora nervous. She was even more unsettled by being on the second floor for the first time in weeks. It did not feel rebellious when she was on her own. It felt foolishly irresponsible. If she was the target, she was a moving target when she moved about the building, bringing it closer to the sweet, unknowing old woman. Nora knocked on the door and called out to Gail to ensure she was all right before moving on to Ezra's.

"Is that you, Nora, dear?" Gail cheerfully called out from within.

"Yes, ma'am, it's me. Are you all right in there?" Nora put her hand on the knob, wondering if she should open it further or pull it shut.

"Oh, I am as right as rain, my sweet girl! Don't stand there like a wolf, my dear. Come in! Come in!" she insisted.

Pushing open the door, she passed a large, gilded cage filled with songbirds that chirped happily as she moved further into the apartment. Turning a corner, she found more feathers drifting down to the floor, being pushed about with a broom by Gail. The small woman danced happily about in the center of the living room. Catching sight of her, the breath caught in Nora's throat, and she fought against the twinkles that drifted in her eyes, signally that she was about to faint.

Putting a hand on the wall beside her to steady herself, she took in the sight of her neighbor. Broom in hand, she spun about, sweeping up large, silvery grey feathers that had slipped from the actual wings that protruded from her back. Spreading out at least four feet on each side of her demure body, they haphazardly knocked over knickknacks on shelves and a tall lamp in the corner as she moved.

"I guess this is quite the sight to you, dear. Well, moving on. Make yourself useful and pass me that dustpan."

CHAPTER
ELEVEN

XX
JUDGEMENT.

Nora stood frozen against the wall, eyes locked on the winged woman before her, unable to speak. Gail was small in a delicate way, less than five feet tall, and thin as a rail. She had silver hair, straight as a pin, that was sharply parted down the middle and snipped bluntly at her shoulders to frame shining emerald eyes that were sharper than you would think for someone who looked to be in her eighties, at least. One would consider her birdlike if they were to pass her on the street, even without the wings that she now exposed through perfectly sized holes in the back of her worn floral house dress. Giving them a shuffle, she tucked them in along her back. It seemed impossible that her little body could even support their weight with the density of the feathers.

"Sorry for the mess. I'm cleaning up for a visitor this afternoon," Gail said in a bluster as if the housework was more shocking than her grand reveal to Nora, "One other than you, that is. Don't get me wrong. You're a very welcome guest as well," she added, picking up the dustpan that Nora was too shocked to pass to her and attempted to shuffle the debris onto it, and instead spread the pile further across the floor. She looked up to Nora, "Would you mind, dear?"

She moved unsteadily to take the pan from her and squat down beside the dusty feathers. Gail started to make progress with the clean-up while Nora took in the sight of the neatly folded wings on her neighbor's back. The soft, grey undertones were broken up with metallic tips of golds and silvers that made intricate paths of shimmering threads that led back up to her body. The morning sunlight lit them up with a soft, warm glow that was nearly hypnotizing. Everything else about her was the same as she had always been. The wings were definitely new, and Nora had no idea how she had been able to conceal them. She would not have missed that, no matter how many strange things she had been exposed to.

"Are you," Nora paused, unable to believe she was asking it as a serious question, "an angel?"

"An angel? Well, I would like to think of myself as one, as we all do," she laughed musically and took the full dustpan from Nora's shaking hand, "but I like gossip and whiskey in my tea, a little too much to think I'll get that job."

Nora watched her carefully carry the pan from the room and heard the squeak of a garbage can lid before the woman returned empty-handed. She sat on a plastic-covered sofa and set her small, slippered feet on the heavy coffee table in front of her.

"How do you have those? Sorry, but how can you have wings?" Nora asked, quickly sitting when the elderly woman motioned for her to sit beside her in a worn wingback chair. She wracked her brain for any beings that would have wings that were not an angel. She had been told that there were many more types of supernaturals than vampires that called Aumbry Valley home, even though she had only come in contact with a few. Whatever Gail was, she had not even seen in the movies.

"How do I have hands and feet, and what used to be the best bazongas in the valley? It's how I was born, darling!" she let out a hearty laugh, "I did get my wings before the boobs, I suppose," she looked down the neck hole of her smock dress and sighed, "At least my wings defied gravity. Although I guess that's their purpose, aren't they?"

Her friendly, light demeanor somehow calmed Nora's nerves more quickly than she expected, and she could steady her voice even as her body still trembled, "I'm sorry, I don't know how to ask this, but what are you?" Nora asked, feeling bad that she could not think of another way of phrasing it that would be less blunt. In the moment, it was good enough even to be able to speak.

"Other than fabulous, fun, and feathered?" she beamed, "I'm a peri, dear."

"A peri? I've never heard of those. Oh, I'm sorry - *of you*. Of what you are," Nora confessed in a squeaking, nervous voice. The supernatural education of Nora Goodman looked to be never-ending.

"From what I've heard, sweetie, you haven't heard of a lot of things in the valley. Yet here we all are. Living our lives," Gail said with gusto before giving Nora a soft look of compassion, "It must be a lot for a little mortal to take in. Especially with all of your troubles," she continued when Nora stayed silent, "A peri is a super natured, dear, just like everything else that finds their way to this place. Well, most that do. I spent a couple of centuries bumping around and making myself useful, having a grand time, but there comes a time when the shine comes off the watch, and it ticks a little slower. That's a time to settle into a nest and have a nice rest. I found this valley and made Dunhope Manor my cozy little retirement nest."

She said it so plainly that it almost made her wings look like they weren't out of place on her tiny, slightly hunched back. Nora leaned in towards her, "Does anyone else know?"

Gail leaned forward as well, "A lot of people do," she winked and sat back, "Around these parts, you're the weirdo, sweetheart," she smiled when Nora frowned, "I don't say that to be cruel. It's just the plain old mortals around these parts are treated like worker ants or supper. It's not often we have one living among us. Two at that, including that sweet spoonful of jam next door," she raised her eyebrows playfully, "When am I getting him back, anyways? You've been hogging him lately. I bet he'd like a peek at these. Do you think he's into feathers?"

Nora smiled at the saucy look the woman directed her way but shrugged and moved on, "Do Jenny and Norman know?"

"Of course, Jenny knows. She was one of the ones that insisted that I keep my wings bundled up and squished to keep you and the sugar-butt next door comfortable.

As for Norman, Norman knows what Norman knows. Has he seen the wings? No idea. Who knows what someone who leaves their house once a month knows? I shouldn't be cruel, but he's just strange, you know? He's so jittery. So secretive. I don't trust that sort. Anyways, it doesn't matter. Now that I've heard through the grapevine that you've been left on your own, I figure you're settled in enough for me to relax in my own home again, and I'm loving it! If we have fae and demons trotting around the place and vampires floating about having window-side chat-fest, why should I keep myself strapped up anymore? You're going to be a long-hauler here, I can tell. You can handle me in all my glory. It's a shame to keep these beauties under wraps. The wings, not the bazongas. Well, not the bazongas anymore."

Nora didn't know how to respond to a woman with wings calling someone else strange. Being told she seemed like someone who would stay in that crazy town was even more unsettling. The stranger things became, the more she was looking forward to leaving. Gail was a sweet lady, definitely not a threat, but Nora had come to miss the monotony of her plain vanilla life from which she had been running. When she told herself she needed to start remembering how to get out and live her life again, she had not considered that she was still in Aumbry Valley and not out in the world that she had arrived from. The citizens of that town were anything but plain vanilla.

"I don't think I would ever get used to living here. Like you said, being a plain old mortal makes me a little out of place," she confessed.

"You'd be surprised what becomes home when you least expect it. You stay around the valley long enough, and it grows roots in you. It keeps what it likes, Nora," Gail said ominously yet with a smile.

Nora thought of the idea of a place holding onto someone, unease settling into the edge of her nerves. The woman sat quietly, her friendly eyes set on her visitor as if everything was perfectly normal. Nora reminded herself that to Gail, everything was normal. They sat in awkward silence while she tried to process the newest shock of the day. As if her brain had finally reached its limit of the unbelievable showing itself to her, a numbness started to overtake her. A jingle of keys in the hallway reminded her why she had stopped on the second floor. "Oh, Ezra," she stood from the seat.

"Oh, dear, my hair is a wreak! I don't want him to see me not put together. You go on now and let me finish cleaning up for my visitor. We can have a proper chat and a tea another time," she whisked Nora towards the door, opening it and giving her a shove, staying hidden, and clicking the door closed.

Nora stood stiff in the hallway, feathers drifting around her from the breeze that escaped from the slamming door behind her.

"Were you just visiting with Gail?" Ezra asked, walking from his apartment doorway, "I thought he hated having people in her place?"

"I was...I," Nora turned for the stairs and moved towards Jenny's apartment, attempting to find the words the entire way.

"Nora, are you okay? What happened?" Ezra repeatedly asked, worried by her seemingly catatonic state. He matched her steps and, thankfully, took her arm to get her safely to the main floor of the building. She needed all the help she could get to stay on her feet.

When they walked into the apartment and the warm, comforting scent of breakfast being made, Jenny only had to look at the expression on her face and the feathers that had settled in her hair to know what was wrong.

"So, you finally met Gail, huh? I mean, you met *all* of her?" Jenny grinned and handed her a mimosa, "Here, you'll need a couple of these."

"What's that supposed to mean? What's up with Gail?" Ezra questioned them, irked when Nora responded only by downing her drink and holding her glass out for a second, and Jenny only laughed and refilled it.

Nora sipped quietly, still processing the discovery, while Jenny, with the help of Olivia, let Ezra in on Gail's well-kept secret.

"No fuuuu...reaking way!" Ezra exclaimed, stopping his first reaction when he looked at Olivia's little face watching him, "Gail's a bird-lady? This place just gets crazier and crazier."

Nora gulped the mimosa and held out her glass for a third. Jenny was right; many more would be required.

"She's a peri, Ezra. She has the most pretty wings of all the wings in the world," Olivia cheered, holding out her arms as if she had a set of her own and running around the room as if in flight, "I want wings like that when I grow up."

"I've never heard of that. What's a peri?" Ezra asked, grabbing himself a drink.

Jenny pulled another bottle of prosecco from her fridge and set it in front of a still-wordless Nora, "You better get educated on who actually lives around these parts if you're seriously thinking of joining a crew here, Ezra. You are well aware that there's a lot more than vampires out there."

"I guess that's an understatement," Ezra croaked.

"Well, I guess a peri is sort of like a cupid. I think that's the most basic way to say it. They have dealings with love and that sort of thing. It's a much more complicated thing than a baby with an arrow and a diaper, in any case. They're most famous for being pranksters, so I'm not surprised she chose to reveal herself to Nora in a way that left her in this state," Jenny snickered.

"I did not see that coming," Nora managed to say, "I guess that's what your high priestess was talking about, huh?"

"I doubt Priestess Maren would worry much over little 'ol Gail," Jenny objected, "She keeps to herself, mostly."

"She said she was cleaning up for a visitor?" Nora remembered, "I thought no one could get into the building without you guys knowing?" Nora quickly wanted the comfort and security that her prison upstairs provided, even if that security was only in her mind.

Jenny took Nora's hand to reassure her, "They can't, Nora. Don't worry about it. Gail's a little squirrely. She's probably talking about a flock of pigeons or something."

"Crows would be more appropriate," Ezra joked.

"Or bats!" Olivia chimed in, still flapping her invisible wings.

Nora ate breakfast as quickly as she could and took the stairs back up two at a time when she was done. Passing Norman's door, she wondered how much he knew. If he were aware of the insanity that existed all around them, it would certainly explain why he stayed shut away in his apartment.

Locking the door behind her, she turned on the tv and flicked through the guide until her mind emptied. Her first casual venture out was less carefree than she had hoped.

CHAPTER TWELVE

Davina, the head honcho, just below Elijah, for the BITN crews in the area, and her right-hand man Dan did not take long to sweep Ezra into their fold when he agreed to sign on with them. He jumped in head first and was glowing with purpose right from his first day of training. On the other hand, Nora found herself retreating further away from anything outside her apartment. When alone, she was confronted with her private thoughts that would tell her that she was doing more damage than benefit by hiding away from the world. She lied to herself and said that as soon as Quinn was captured again, she would leave the valley behind and head back east.

Alone.

Just catch her again, and I'm out of here.

She would give herself a do-over of her breaking free from her lonely life that had run from. The same lies she had told herself before there was the hope of leaving peacefully. She let herself float freely in the pink cloud she created. Time passed by dreaming up different scenarios that could be her life outside Dunhope Manor. Sometimes she pictured herself back-packing across Europe, sometimes a simple job in a simple cubicle in a simple, supernatural-free town. Knowing what she now knew, she knew there was little chance that some form of supernatural being wouldn't be in any place she settled.

With Ezra training at night and sleeping during the day and Jenny rarely around due to the time she needed to spend with her coven, Nora usually found herself alone. Even Olivia had stopped visiting as much. Nora told herself it was because Ezra's sleeping made it hard to have fun during the day, but she knew that her gloomy mood kept the little girl away. It was easy to sense, even without the extrasensory abilities she was told Olivia had. It didn't help that Jenny had decided to keep Olivia's birthday minimal, having a mommy-daughter day instead of the party she had hoped for. Nora felt guilty that the darkness in her heart was starting to spread over Dunhope Manor.

The vibrant red dye had officially been rinsed away, and her hair was once again a simple, mousey brown. She did not see the warm gingerbread that Ezra said it was. The bold new, take-charge Nora that arrived in Aumbry Valley in search of Quinn was returning to the mode of quiet girl on the sidelines who was practically invisible to the world. The lost, sad girl she had been when she was in school. While Ezra was blooming and thriving, Nora was losing direction. The only thing they had in common anymore was the mark the fae had made on the inside of their wrists. The impossible gold shimmer down the center was the only sparkle Nora had left. She scrubbed at it in the shower every morning, wishing it away. There was no place for her there, and she wanted no reminder of another place she did not fit in.

Within a few days of Ezra's official start with the crew, they had fallen into a new routine in the apartment. Nora was glad he had decided to stay in the apartment with her. Being left alone anymore with her own thoughts would drive her mad. Ezra would be gone all night, deep into his training, and then sleep away the exhaustion all day. He had taken to sleeping in Nora's bed to free up the couch during the day, even though he could easily sleep in his own bed in his own apartment. Even though they barely saw each other outside of meals, it was nice to know someone was there. The space felt warmer when she wasn't alone. Silas was also happy, having someone to snuggle with in bed day and night, and he would only pop up from the bed to use his litter or get something to eat. Nora warned him that he was going to get chubby, but the grey fluffball only stretched and returned to the comfort of her duvet.

They would eat breakfast and dinner together each day, as they did before, but the conversations became stilted when Ezra spent the first few days trying to talk Nora into joining the crew along with him. The image of Jude's body exploding into hot ash and drifting about her was still raw in her mind. Putting herself in a position of possibly having to do that again wasn't high on her list of goals, let alone giving a life pledge to work for them. The roots of the valley were growing within him, and Nora only felt pushed away from it.

A couple of weeks into her spiral of depression, she admitted to herself that she was making excuses to be miserable. Ezra was making the best of the situation and was moving on with his life. Nora was turning into

Norman, shut away from the world and frozen in time. She did not know why Norman lived as he did. It became clear to her that she was choosing to hide away and feel sorry for herself. She knew Elijah and the bureau depositing money in her account was one of the excuses she clung to. The comfort of her financial needs being cared for was one that she knew well and had missed in her few months on her own. Leaving it behind would mean stepping up and taking care of her responsibilities. One of the main reasons she had hit the road in the first place. Since she didn't ask to be a part of their mess or become an enemy of Quinn's, she would allow herself to accept the money for a short while more as long as she was honest with herself about what it was to be used for. It was sustaining her until she found the will and the way to leave, and they did not seem to mind being generous.

She didn't know what she wanted to do with the rest of her life, but she knew it would not be in Aumbry Valley. Dunhope Manor would not be her forever home, especially one she was trapped in. Just because she had been marked forever by the fae, she told herself she owed them nothing. The supernatural beings had used her for their needs and failed at the task at that, and they were done with her now. A fire started to burn within her when she stopped feeling sorry for herself. Leaving behind Ezra and the friends she had made was the only thought that would bring her down again, so she pushed it down deep inside. She knew that it would have to be for good when she left. Whether Quinn was still out there or not, she would have to leave and never return. She couldn't let *what-ifs* freeze her in place. Whatever Quinn was trying to do, she would do it no matter where Nora was.

Gail was right about the valley growing roots inside of the ones it wanted to keep. Nora didn't want to risk that happening to her as it seemed to have happened to her friends. She would leave while it was still pushing her out. The up and down of emotions was overwhelming, yet it was better than the numbness that was trying to regain its hold. She wondered if that was the metaphorical grip of the valley seeping into her mind. If it was, they had a much more pleasant planting within Ezra. He could not stop smiling. Nora pushed aside her jealousy and was glad to see him happily throw himself into something for the first time since *The Night*. It was interesting to listen to him go on about the various beings who dwelled within Aumbry as he learned of them, especially the sort she had never heard of. She was surprised to be told of the many different types of fae or that multiple packs of werewolves lived up in the posh houses of the hills where Quinn's vampire nest had been. It was equally fascinating and a push to get the hell out there out of there.

Another help to Nora's mood was Gabriel, who had made a point to have a quick window visit and check in with Nora each night after Ezra had left to train. She admitted to her decision to leave when he commented on how nice it was to see her spirit being up. He did not like her choice, even if he understood why, and he certainly disapproved of her leaving when Quinn was still out wreaking havoc. He reiterated his feelings during each visit after her confession. When he arrived, he brought her more extravagate gifts of wine, art, and, strangely, coins in hopes of bribing her to stay.

His latest gift was a bottle of French wine with a delicate illustration of a castle on the label. It looked like it belonged in the wine cellar of a billionaire rather than being sipped by a woman sitting cross-legged on an unmade bed with her hair in a messy bun and rips in her pajama pants. Nora knew it probably came from the former, who was most likely someone Gabriel had been snacking on. The flavor explosion with the first sip was worth the image that came to mind when she poured the deep, red wine into her glass. The gentle buzz started warm in her belly and rose to her cheeks by the second glass.

"You have to know, it's nothing against you or any of the crazy beings that live here," Nora said with a sigh.

Gabriel had his own glass that he brought for their gabfests that he refilled from an ancient-looking flask. Nora pretended it was also wine when he took a big swallow before he spoke, "Like being a mortal is so normal. It's not normal, Nora, it's boring," he sniffed.

"Well, I miss boring. I know I complained a lot about my parents and growing up in their stuffy world. I guess stuffy and boring mean safe to me now. This place is starting to mess with my head, Gabriel. I can't keep my moods even, you know? One minute I'm depressed and angry; the next, I'm numb. The only thing that has been keeping me positive is the final decision to leave," Nora pulled a fluffy fleece blanket onto her lap against the chill breezing in through the window. Silas curled up against her, and she tangled her fingers in his soft fur, "Nothing is going to be the same anymore, no matter where I go, so why do I have to stay here? My mind isn't wired to handle the things that go on here. The things that live here. It's too much."

Gabriel mulled over her words, "So, do you think you'll go back to them?"

"Who? My parents?" Nora gave a tired laugh at the idea, "I'm twenty-four - actually twenty-five in just a few weeks - I didn't graduate college, and I have no job options or any discernible skills. Going home to them is just too sad to add to that list."

"Then stay. Fuck all of this *too much* bullshit!" Gabriel said with a flourish, "You tell me stories of all of the adventures you had with your grandfather and the strange places you went to, and you're telling me the one place that has brought you friendship and security is too much? Stop moping about this crappy apartment and get on with it. You can have a life here. You're wasting away in there waiting to live your life, girl. I miss the little spitfire I met. I'm sorry to say it, but you're getting boring in there."

Nora swung her legs over to sit on the side of her bed, staring at the vampire outside her window who stared right back, "You're right about that," she looked about the room, and her eyes landed on the polaroid photos she had taped up above her headboard. Smiling snapshots of her with the people that had become her family. "I keep thinking of the connections I've made here that will be painful to lose, and it makes me want to stay. When it comes down to it, I don't think I belong here. I'm just hiding away from everything out there. There has to be somewhere that danger isn't the first thing I think of when I wake up and go to sleep."

"Danger? Fuck danger, Nora. Danger is waiting around every corner wherever you go. It's a non-issue. At least here, you have people who look out for you. More importantly, imagine the birthday party I could throw you!"

A jingle at the door had Nora on her feet and Gabriel as close to the window as the charms would allow. The buzz of the wine sobered when her heart was palpitated with adrenaline in response to the noise. No one would be visiting this close to midnight. No one with good intentions, at least. She grabbed the silver-tipped stake that she kept on her dresser and crept towards her bedroom door. The last lock clicked open as Nora rushed to press against the wall beside the entry.

As soon as it swung open, she launched and found herself lifted into the air and quickly down onto her back, flat on the floor. The stake was twisted from her hand, and she heard it bounce against the wall across the room. The speed of the takedown knocked the wind from her, and she struggled against the hand that held her down.

"What the hell, Nora?" Ezra's voice rang out loudly.

Nora gulped in the air, coughing as she was helped to sit up, "Ezra? What are you doing here?"

He knelt beside her, his hand on her back, "What do you mean? I still live here, don't I?"

"Yeah, of course," Nora struggled to her feet, "I mean, what are you doing here now? You've only been gone a few hours."

"Some of the newbies were given the Ascension tonight, so we got to go home early," he said, looking her over for injury.

"Did they give it to you again?" Nora asked, remembering how terrified she was during hers. The creepy strapped chair, Gabriel's fangs shining in the dim light, the shimmering serum in the frighteningly large syringe. It seemed like forever and a day since that moment, yet the fear was still fresh.

"No, not the whole shebang this time. They did give me another shot of that super-fairy juice, as you can tell," Ezra laughed, flexing his bicep, before helping Nora to the chair, "Sorry about that, by the way. You remember how those instincts are," he apologized.

"Yeah, and I apparently don't have them anymore," she moaned and rubbed at her lower back, "Is it a good idea to take that with what Elijah told us? It's deadly with a vampire bite."

"Like I said, I'd rather be dead than a vamp. Hey, check this out!" Ezra exclaimed, kneeling in front of the chair and rolling up his sleeve to expose the mart they were given. The charcoal ankh and glimmering metallic stripe down the middle now had a thicker band of gold in the center and what looked like a circle of silver set at the base. It sparkled even brighter than the single stripe they both had, as if gold dust and platinum had been implanted into his arm. She reached out to run her fingers along it and only felt his warm, smooth skin.

"Is everything okay?" a quiet voice came from beyond the open door in the hallway. Norman peered inside.

"Yeah, sorry for the commotion, Norman," Nora said, rising from the chair, "Ezra just startled me. We're all good here."

Norman kept his eyes on Ezra, trailing down to the arm branding that he quickly covered, "All right. Have a good night," he murmured and retreated behind his door.

"What a strange dude," Ezra chuckled. He was on an even stronger high of happiness than he had been yet.

"I think it's a stretch calling him strange around here," Nora said, pulling two bottles of water from the fridge and tossing one to Ezra with a grunt. The strain she felt let her know she had pulled something in her back. The accuracy and strength of her throw let her know all of the fae serum had not left her system, and the twinge of pain let her know there wasn't much left. Ezra gave an approving nod to the toss.

"True. Seeing as how we have a witch as a landlady and bird lady as a neighbor," Ezra said, twisting the bottle open.

"She's a peri, not a bird lady," Gabriel called out from Nora's bedroom.

Ezra jumped, on alert, "Who's in the bedroom?"

"I completely forgot Gabriel's here for a visit!" Nora exclaimed and went back to join him at the window. Ezra trailed behind her, a scowl of disappointment at the visit creeping onto his face.

"They're actually very rare gals and so much fun when they're in their prime," Gabriel continued when they sat on the bed to join him.

Nora had looked up peris on the web, along with all of the other types of beings that Ezra spoke of, when the shock of meeting Gail in her true form had lessened. They were blood relatives of angels that were renowned for their beauty. Gail was an older woman, how old Nora couldn't guess, and time had worn her youthful good looks, but even with the silver hair and creased face, Nora could tell she had been a breathtaking woman. Her emerald-green eyes still retained the sparkle of someone who was enjoying life. The idea of an angel's relative choosing Dunhope Manor as their retirement home amused Nora. Gail could go anywhere in the world, possibly even to other worlds, and she chose a stuffy apartment with peeling plaster in Aumbry Valley.

"Fun is one thing you're an expert on, Gabriel," Nora teased.

"You know it," Gabriel winked at her. He leaned forward when he spied the edge of Ezra's branding peeking out from his rolled sleeve, "So, it's true?"

Ezra ran his palm over the inside of his forearm and tugged down the fabric of his shirt, "Uh, yeah. It's true."

"What's true?" Nora asked, looking between the two when tension thickened the air, "What does the added stuff mean?"

"Our Ezra here is becoming a shining star in the BITN Bureau. Everyone in The Firm has been gushing about how brilliant he will be. Mr. Fast-track-to-the-big-leagues," Gabriel said with a bitter edge to each word.

"What? That's awesome! Congrats, Ez!" Nora said, stopping when Ezra looked at Gabriel and then to the floor, "Isn't that good?"

"Mr. Davis, here, is being groomed for the hit squad," Gabriel replied flatly.

"Is that true?" Nora asked with concern. That wasn't just keeping tabs on vampires and the like. That was real danger, and it had been made clear that any mortal who kills a vampire could be disposed of like dirty gloves if they so chose, even if they had been instructed to do so. They had already been lucky enough not to have faced the consequences for the two who had died at their hands. Now Ezra was choosing to go into the belly of the beast, "Do you have a death wish? That's just plain stupid, Ezra."

"It's not what it sounds like," he muttered.

"How is not? That's too dangerous," Nora shouted, standing to stride back and forth across the bedroom floor with frustration.

It was one thing to find purpose. It was another to die for it. She knew it was too late for him to back out; he had made a life pledge to them. Now he was taking the chance of making that pledge a lot shorter.

Ezra spoke without raising his eyes to either of them, "It's not like I'll be out vampire hunting like in the movies. It's all very official."

"It's a dumb move, is what it is," Nora retorted, "Why would you want to risk your life like that? Revenge? You'd risk dying just for revenge?"

Ezra shifted in his seat on the bed, not responding to her questions. His eyes were locked on the floor before him, and his tense jaw twitched. Nora stopped her argument, knowing there was no point. Not only was Ezra stubborn, but it was also his life and his choices. Nora had no right to make any decisions for him, especially if she planned to leave the valley for good. She chewed lightly on the inside of her cheek to keep herself from continuing her reprimand. Gabriel watched the two sit in uncomfortable silence before turning on his fang-framed dazzling smile in an attempt to move on from the news, "Well, we were just talking about what will be the next fun chapter in Nora's life, right Nora?"

"What do you mean?" Ezra turned to her, "What next chapter?"

"I don't know. I don't know exactly what. Just that I need to do something. I can't just sit in this apartment waiting for something to happen," Nora sat on the opposite side of the bed, feeling like it was her turn to be scolded.

"So, are you going to join the crew?" Ezra smiled broadly for a split second until Nora turned unamused eyes to him.

"No, not *that*," she stressed, "I honestly don't know exactly. All I know is that I've decided that I have to leave here. Leave Aumbry Valley for good."

Ezra slapped his hand on the bed, upset at her revelation, "And go where? Quinn is still out there."

Nora rubbed at a headache that was starting to spread, "Quinn will always be out there, Ezra."

"Not always," Ezra said bitterly and changed his tone when he saw the hurt look on Nora's face, "Sorry, but...she's a threat to everyone. Can't you wait and see what happens? Please give it a bit. You can't just go running off."

"That's all I have been doing, Ez. Running away from the life I was living to sit here and see what horror will happen next. I need to start living my life. I feel like a ghost floating around in this apartment. I'm living on memories and fear. This place is going to make me go mad if I stay."

"You don't have to leave to live your life," Ezra said firmly, "I know how you feel. I do. I was a ghost of myself when I lost Rose and Adalyn. I just drifted through day after day. I didn't have a reason to get up in the morning, or even a reason to smile, no matter how many times I plastered a grin on my face to get through it for other people's sake. I'll be honest, when I first came here, when I first found out about," he bobbed his head towards Gabriel, "what this place was...when I found out about Jude, I think you were right. I did have a death wish. I really did. I didn't care what happened to me."

"I get that. You went through a huge trauma. I can't even imagine how painful that was," Nora consoled and moved to sit at his side.

"My point is that's who I was. I've become someone else here, someone who is living, not just existing. A lot of that is because of you," he cleared his throat and quickly continued, "Because of the friends we've made and the world we've started to create around us. You can do that here, too. You don't have to leave to find out what you want. This place is as good as any, with Quinn out there threatening to destroy the world as we know it. You might find exactly what you want your future to be right here while we have the chance."

"Nora and Emo-zra are dropping emotional truth bombs all over the place tonight," Gabriel squealed, making the two jump in their seats, "I think he's right, though, Nora. I'd miss you too much, you warm little blood bag. We all would."

"I still think I need to get out of here," Nora contested.

"Out of this shitty apartment, not out of our lives," Gabriel rolled his eyes, "You mortals are so dramatic," he smiled wickedly and pushed himself back from the windowsill, "Anyways, you two talk amongst yourselves. I'm getting snacky so I'm going to find something tall, dark, and warm to sip on," he purred and left in a blink.

"Ew," Ezra sniped, "So gross."

Nora stood to shut the window, giving a quick scan of the empty street below, and they made their way out to the kitchen.

Ezra noticed the bottle of wine in her hands and grabbed himself a glass from the kitchen before holding it out for her to share, "I hope you don't think I'm being pushy about wanting you to stay. I know you don't want to join the crew. I won't ask you to again. I promise."

"It's not that. It's not any one thing. You were just as keen to leave before you found a purpose. If I'm being honest, I don't want anything to do with supernatural beings ever again. Maybe it would be best to have my mind wiped, and I can start over," Nora said, knowing that it would be even more dangerous not to be aware of what was around her. It was the last few months of her life and what they contained that she wanted to disappear completely. She watched Ezra sip the wine and smile with an appreciation for it and conceded that not everything needed to disappear from her memories.

Ezra swallowed another mouthful of the pricey wine and sat in his spot on the couch, "That won't change the fact that everything we've learned about here would still be real."

"They do say ignorance is bliss," Nora breathed, pouring herself another glass.

Ezra switched the TV on and found where they had left off on their latest love-struck hot mess of a reality show they had been watching, "These dummies kind of prove your point, I guess," he said, pointing to the tv, "They seem pretty blissful."

Nora laughed and slid over to make room for Silas to snuggle between them. It had been some time since they had a fun roomies night, and Nora allowed herself to empty her mind of worries and enjoy the moment. After all, Ezra would be gone again the next night to get back to training.

Training to kill vampires.

Nora had to push that thought away hard to silence it for the night. The beginning of an ending was in the air around them, and they ignored it as best they could. What all would end was what frightened her most.

A new day lay ahead, and she would set out a plan when it came. Until then, she would enjoy the brief moment of happiness while she had it.

CHAPTER THIRTEEN

It was a pleasant surprise when Jenny knocked on her door with Olivia in tow. Her mood had been improving in the last few days, and the little girl was starting to enjoy visiting again. Her smile to the pair did not last long when she saw they were deep into a mother-daughter battle. Jenny looked as if she was at the end of her rope with the precocious little mop top.

"If I have to tell you again, Olivia, you'll be spending the evening in your room!" Jenny shouted with the painful frustration reserved for parents of little ones. Jenny let Nora know that Olivia had spent the majority of the day insisting on going to the ballroom to visit her invisible friend, the dancing girl. The tantrums had burned themselves out into a constant whine that was eating away at her frazzled mother. Nora offered to take her off her hands for a playdate and dinner to give Jenny a couple of hours of peace, much to Jenny's appreciation. Between the coven convening in her apartment and Olivia becoming stir-crazy, there hadn't been much time for Jenny to have any time to herself. Since time was something that Nora had in spades, as long as she stayed in town, she felt it was only fitting to share it.

"But I have to, mommy! The mean lady's gonna come get her and take her away again. She doesn't want to go with her. She wants to stay, and I told her she can share my room," Olivia pleaded. She turned to Nora, hoping for an ally in her fight. Nora stayed neutral-faced and on the outside of the argument.

"Now she's giving free room and bored to invisible friends," Jenny sighed, "If she wants to live here, she can come down on her own. You're not going to convince me to let you go up there. It's too dangerous, and it's off limits, missy."

"Come on, Olivia, don't ruin our fun day. Ezra's even said he was getting up early today. That will give you guys time to watch that doggy cop show you love," Nora coaxed.

"Doggy cop show? Oh, Norma, you don't get our shows, do you?" Olivia giggled, her mood brightening at the prospect of the visit. She gave her mother an ice-cold glare for good measure and bounded off in search of Silas.

"I really don't, cutie. Sorry," Nora called out to her, "But at least I'm good at making the popcorn."

Jenny thanked Nora for the break and repeated instructions to Olivia to behave as she headed back down the stairs. Nora turned to find Olivia propping up the two dolls she had toted up against an unimpressed Silas, who had come out of the bedroom to inspect the visitors. She sat beside them and noticed a silvery feather in Olivia's ponytail and pulled it out to turn it over in the light, making it shimmer.

"Do you know Gail well?" Nora asked, still amazed with how much the little girl was aware of and able to take with a grain of salt. Growing up in the middle of it all would give her the benefit of not knowing how unusual her town was compared to others.

"I guess. She's pretty funny. I'm not allowed in her apartment, though. She says I'm too *runbunching* and would get her birds going coo-coo," she answered, using her fingers to rake through a doll's hair.

"You're *runbunching?*" Nora repeated the word in her head until she figured it out, "Do you mean rambunctious?" Nora asked, holding in a laugh.

Olivia put a finger to her chin while she thought it over, "Yeah, that's it," she nodded and started to primp the second doll, "But that's okay. I like her friend better. She comes to see me in my apartment."

Nora picked up the little ballerina doll she had set aside, fussing with the pale pink tutu she wore, "Who's her friend?" she asked, wondering if that's whom Gail had meant was visiting when she was in her apartment. Jenny had said no one got in without anyone knowing. She worried that if Olivia was as advanced as Jenny had implied, there was a chance she was able to allow someone in.

Olivia looked up at Nora with a happy grin, "Pearl! Oh, I like her. She's a nice lady, but she smells like cigarettes and asks too many questions sometimes."

Nora stopped straightening the doll's dress and gave Olivia her full attention.

Pearl? Smells like cigarettes?

Nora knew precisely who that was but didn't understand why she would be visiting Jenny and Olivia.

She was also a little hurt that she would come all the way over to Dunhope Manor and not pop up to say hello to her. They weren't close, but they were friendly, and Nora was only one floor up from Gail's apartment if she had already come that far.

"Does Pearl come to visit you and your mom a lot?" Nora asked. How many people were coming in and out of that building that she didn't know about? It did not give her faith that the building was as secure as she had been told.

"She doesn't visit mommy. Just me. She poofs in my room sometimes," Olivia made her fingers look like a little explosion.

"Poofs? She poofs?" Nora could not translate the toddler meaning of that.

"Yeah. She's not there, and then poof!" she popped her fingers again, "Her cloud poofs into my room, and then she's there," Olivia explained. Before she could ask a follow-up question, Ezra shuffled out of the bedroom, rubbing the sleep from his eyes with a balled fist.

"Hey, buddy, how ya doing?" he asked happily when he saw their visitor. She tossed her dolls onto Nora's lap and ran to give his legs a tight hug. Ezra smiled and patted her head, "Looks like I'm up just in time for our show. Maybe we can talk Nora into making the little noodles we like for dinner, too," he said, turning a puppy dog pout to Nora. Olivia mirrored him with a mischievous giggle.

"Miss. Olivia here was just telling me how she gets visits from Pearl in her room," Nora said slowly to Ezra.

"Pearl? Elijah's secretary?" he asked, confused, "Why?"

Nora was glad that he found it strange as well. He was getting so much information through his training, and she worried that he would start to keep things from her like everyone else. The questioning look on his face told her he was still not being told everything. Just like she wasn't.

"She likes to ask about how everyone is. She says I'm the eyes and ears of this place because I'm the only one who pays attention," Olivia said with pride, "Pearl likes to know what's going on, and I know *everything* around here."

"And she poofs into her room," Nora added with raised eyebrows, over-annunciating the words.

"Poofs?" Ezra repeated and looked at Olivia, "And what does that mean?"

"You know, her cigarette smoke comes in my room, and then poof! There she is," Olivia described as if she was explaining to morons how to put bread in a toaster, "She poofs!"

Ezra and Nora shared a look of bewilderment. Ezra brought the girl by the hand to the couch, and they sat down on either side of her. This was another new one for them.

"Any idea what that means," Nora asked Ezra, "Anything like that come up in your training?"

He frowned with an uneasy laugh, "People *poofing*? No, I can't say that it has. We pretty well stick to vamp info. Not a thing that can *poof*."

"That's rude, Ezra. Pearl isn't a thing. She's a ghost lady, geez," Olivia admonished, slapping his leg.

Nora thought of the sight of Pearl the first day she encountered her in the dingy front office of 1365 Beech Avenue. Thanks to the cigarette smoke that filled the room, Nora was sure her eyes were playing tricks on her. For a moment, Pearl appeared to be slightly translucent. Ezra's expression told her that he seemed to have the same recollection. Sweet little old Pearl was a spirit of some sort. When they met, she had said she had worked for Elijah Beasley *for centuries*. There's a good chance that she wasn't exaggerating the timeline.

"So, she's a ghost?" Nora prodded further. A ghost would be the least shocking entity she had been exposed to since her arrival. Jenny had told her that there were not any ghosts in the building. Olivia may be more in the know of what was going on than her mother. Having a four-year-old with more information than everyone else made Nora uneasy.

Olivia picked up her dolls, bored with the line of questioning. She answered them with her eyes on the television, "Pretty much. She says she came here. Didn't you see her?"

Nora looked to the corner of the room, "The white fog I saw!" If it had been Pearl, she was glad it was not another fright created by her mind. It also felt very violating to know that she could poof in unannounced whenever she wanted. Nora found herself sitting back on the couch anxiously as she stared at where the misty fog had appeared.

Ezra's eyes followed hers, "Oh man, that is so creepy," his lips twisted with the thought of the intrusion.

"Why has she been coming here if she doesn't even, I don't know, even just say hi?" Nora asked, scanning the room for any sign of the ghostly mist's arrival. Everything looked as it always did.

"I dunno," Olivia said, entirely over the conversation, and her attention transferred to the cartoon that blasted from the tv, "She was probably looking for something. She's nosey like that."

The eerie feeling of being watched made her reach into her pocket for the obsidian stone Sarah had given her. It may be a placebo effect, or it may be real; either way, she wanted every talisman she could get. If there was one group of supernaturals that she could trust, she knew she could trust the witches.

Switching to her other pocket, she didn't find the stone. Remembering the last time she saw it, the hallucination of the spiders and the fall that followed came to mind. She realized that she hadn't taken the stone from the pocket of her robe since, and it was now hung on the hook in her bedroom. Scurrying quickly to retrieve it, she turned it over in her hand, looking at the spot in her room where she was sure she had witnessed the mist appear. A worry that if what she saw wasn't imagined, then maybe the spiders had been something more than just an imagined threat. A headache started to nag in her temples when she thought of the disturbing moment. She reached up and ran her fingers over the faint scar left on her head. The fae blood still in her system healed the gash well, but she hoped it was finally gone so there wasn't a chance of the experience happening again. If that's what had even caused it. She gripped the obsidian stone tightly in her fist as if she could squeeze any protective powers from it directly into her body.

"Hey, Ez? Do you think this thing really..." Nora's question was cut off when she slammed into the floor. The shock held her in place for a moment until she could push herself up. A razor-thin splinter of wood was twisted up from the hardwood floor and had snagged her sock, slicing into the sole of her foot, "Ow!" she cried as she twisted herself from it. A small drop of blood spread out across her sock.

Ezra moved to her side to help her up. He suppressed a laugh when he saw the tiny sliver that tripped her up, "What are the odds of that? You're getting as klutzy as I used to be. Maybe we should see about getting you more serum."

Olivia popped off of the couch and picked up the stone that had slipped from Nora's hand when she fell. Her face fell, anger brewing in her eyes when so looked it over, "Why do you have this?"

Nora hobbled over to a kitchen chair to tug off her sick to inspect the wound, "It's an obsidian stone. It's supposed to help keep me safe."

Olivia held it up and away from her as if it was spoiled meat, "No, it's not. This is a *moldymate*. This is a very, very bad stone, Norma," Olivia marched to the kitchen and tossed up into the sink. She rushed back to the couch to grab her dolls to keep them away from the offensive stone.

"I'm sorry, Moldymate? What's that? Sarah gave it to me. She said it was obsidian. It's supposed to keep bad things away," Nora said, watching the little girl's anger build. Nora knew that expression and braced herself for an incoming tantrum.

"I told you Sarah was bad, Norma! That's Moldymate. That's for curses and bad luck," she roared, stomping her foot for good measure, "That's a cursed crystal!"

Nora looked at the unassuming green rock and couldn't see how it could have the power to frighten a girl who thought nothing of ghosts and was a talented-beyond-her-years witch. Being a witch, there was a good chance she knew what she was talking about. Nora peered at the inconspicuous, dark green stone in her kitchen sink.

"Sarah wouldn't do that, Olivia. Why would she want to hurt us? She's our friend," Ezra said, trying to calm her as she became more unsettled.

"I'm going to get help. You stay here," Olivia directed, jumping at the locks before he could get to her. She managed to twist two before they became out of reach. She looked to Ezra expectantly before pointing up to the three that remained locked.

"We don't need help, Olivia. It's just a rock. We're ok," Ezra said, pointing to the couch for her to sit, "Let's forget about it and watch our show. You don't need to bother your mom right now."

"No, it's not! It's bad, Ezra. It can hurt her. I need to get help!" the little girl pressed, grim worry creasing her face. She was not going to let it go.

"Okay, well, I'll come down with you then," Ezra said, picking up his phone from the counter to shove in his pocket, "I don't want you running around all upset. *Norma* already had a klutzy fall. I don't want you tumbling down the stairs."

"No, you stay here with her. Please, Ezra, I'll be back in a minute. I promise," she raised her small hands to hold him back from following, "Stay with Norma, okay?"

Ezra heaved a sigh, "Get your mom and come right back here, understand?" he said, giving in to her, as he always did, "And hold the railing!"

"I'll be right back," Olivia promised and was out the door as soon as he opened it for her.

Nora held a paper towel to her foot, the blood already down to a pin drop, "Okay, that was weird, right?" Nora snickered, balling up the ripped sock, "Hopefully, Jenny can sort all of whatever that was out."

"The killer rock is up here, so I'm sure she'll be fine," Ezra laughed, picking the stone up between two fingers before tossing it back into the sink, "When she gets uppity like that, you know only Jenny can calm her down, anyways."

"Why does she hate Sarah so much? She's a nice enough girl," Nora wondered. She waddled to the garbage can to toss the ruined sock, "Maybe she doesn't like how much attention she gives you? She might want to keep you all to herself."

"Who knows? Kids that age rarely make sense," he said with a shake of his head. He pulled out his phone and retook his seat on the sofa, "What did she call it? *Modelmate*?" he asked, typing it out on the keyboard.

Nora joined him on the couch with her own phone out, "No, she said *moldymate*. Who knows what that could actually be," she laughed, "Or if that's even what it's called with the way Olivia pronounces things. I don't know anything about crystals and stuff. I just listened to Sarah because I assumed she knew what she was talking about."

Ezra typed some more and shrugged, "I can't find anything about a cursed moldymate rock. From the lips of babes, huh?" he shook his head with a smile.

Nora stared at her screen, flipping through a few different sites after typing in obsidian. Each photo was of a deeply black, smooth stone, mostly in perfect spheres, "Wait, Sarah said it was obsidian," she turned her screen for him to see, "That doesn't look like what she gave me, at all."

They both turned in the direction of the sink where Ezra had tossed it and stood quickly to take a look again. The jagged green stone didn't look like the screen's photos.

Nora typed quickly into her phone, looking for a cursed green crystal. Pages of different cursed objects scrolled across the screen until one word caught her attention.

Moldavite.

Clicking on the link, an almost perfect match to the stone that sat before them appeared on the screen, and Nora gasped, "Is it just me, or does this look more like what that is?" she asked, comparing the two, not wanting to believe that Olivia had been right.

"Moldavite," Ezra read aloud, "known as the cursed crystal, it can bring about strong emotional feelings, usually confusion and anger, if used against someone with malice."

Nora thought of Ezra's anger when Sarah gave her the stone and how irritated she had become with him. Maybe it wasn't just his disbelief in crystals and magic that had him worked up, and perhaps it wasn't just cabin fever that had caused the bickering. They had been getting along better than ever until that night, and the fighting stopped as soon as she tucked it away in her dresser.

Nora took the phone from him, "Nightmares and intense hallucinations can affect the holder if the charms placed on the crystal have dark intentions," her jaw dropped, "Oh my god. I was holding that thing in my fist when I freaked out in the bathroom!"

Ezra looked at the moldavite sitting harmlessly in front of them, "Come on, Nor. A rock isn't going to make you go crazy. Elijah even said it was probably the serum leaving you. It was messing with your head."

"He said probably. Not for sure, and he didn't know about the stone," Nora said quickly, getting back to the information in her hand, "Moldavite increases the strength in other stones and magical properties," Nora looked to Ezra, "What if it affects fae blood? That could explain the freak-out, couldn't it?"

"I don't know, Nora. Maybe," he said with a tired sigh, heading back to the comfort of the couch, standing beside it when Nora let out an aggravated growl, "I'd be dumb as hell to completely discount it with everything else we've learned, but it just doesn't make sense that Sarah would want to hurt us."

Nora stared at the crystal that was harmlessly glimmering in the sink, "She didn't give it to us, Ez. She gave it to me." Nora's stomach turned.

Ezra stopped in place, "What do you mean?"

"You know exactly what I mean. She gave it to *me*. She wanted to make sure I kept it on *me*."

Ezra shook his head slowly, his eyes narrowing, "Why would she want to hurt you? You're friends."

Nora stepped back from the sink and moved around the kitchen island to his side, "Because she has feelings for you? Maybe she didn't like us hanging around so much. She gave it to me right after you moved in here. Maybe she's just plain nuts and saw me as, I don't know, like a threat or something."

"It was a couple of dates! We had a couple of meals, and that's it. Sarah and I are just friends, and she knows it. You make it seem like we had this epic love story that she can't let go of!" Ezra countered, his voice booming with irritation. He sat down heavily on the couch, his back to her.

Nora let out a forceful exhale, overwhelmed at even the thought of Sarah wanting to harm her, "Maybe she doesn't see it the way you do."

"I don't know. That sounds ridiculous. Sarah doesn't seem like the fatal attraction type. She's so...she's just a quiet, nice girl."

"All I know is we need to tell Jenny. She'll know what's going on," Nora said and pointed with happy relief to the door when a knock announced her arrival, "Trust me, I hope I'm wrong, too. I hope I sound like a complete nutter, and we'll never speak of this again."

Nora opened the door and did not find Jenny standing with Olivia.

The little girl looked up at her with pleading eyes, "Don't be mad, okay? Mommy wouldn't listen, but she knows how bad Sarah is. She can tell you, Norma!" Olivia said softly, holding the hand of a little girl wearing a rumpled tutu and pink leotard. Her soft brown hair tumbled down her back in silky ribbons of curls. Nora stepped back from them when she timidly smiled up at her with two tiny fangs framing her grin. She not only looked familiar, but Nora had also seen her in many photos. Photos that Ezra had shown her.

The tiny vampire leaned towards the apartment's threshold, not crossing to enter. Her quiet voice made Ezra sit up quickly, as stiff as a board when she spoke.

"Hi, Daddy."

CHAPTER FOURTEEN

THE MOON
XVIII

The room stood still around them, not a breath to be heard. Ezra slowly turned his head to see what his ears were telling him was standing at the door to the apartment. When his eyes set sight on what appeared to be his daughter, he jumped and launched himself back, knocking over the coffee table as he stumbled over it.

"This isn't funny," he said, his voice quivering. His eyes scanned manically over the little one whose shy grin was turning into a trembling lip with each second of his horrified reaction.

Olivia let go of her distressed friend's hand and stepped into the room, "It's okay, Ezra. She won't hurt you. She missed you so much," she said, walking in past Nora, who stood in place, her open palm hovering in front of her gaping mouth, "Come on in, Adalyn, it's okay."

"NO!" Nora shouted, too late to stop the invitation from being spoken. She stepped back as the petite vampire crossed into her apartment. Whatever charms had been placed on the building were powerless to the simple words of Olivia. Nora felt herself pressing her back against the cold bricks of her wall, willing herself to pull herself together and deal with the impossible revelation of Adalyn's survival. It was easy to see that she was one of the undead now. Dead or alive, she was very much standing just feet away from her father.

"It can't be," Ezra stepped back for every step she took towards him, his hands held out as if to keep what he saw at bay. The confusion of what his eyes were telling his mind was undoubtedly causing excruciating pain deep within his heart when silent tears slid down his cheek, his face contorted with renewed grief.

"It's me, daddy," Adalyn spoke softly, holding her lip stiffly to cover her fangs, "Please don't cry."

Nora grabbed Olivia by the arm and pulled her against the kitchen wall beside her. Adalyn kept her slow pace towards Ezra, slinking along the shadowed wall, her tiny ballet-shoe-clad feet avoiding the last rays of the setting sun that warmed the floor. His legs shook and gave out, his knees buckling beneath him when she stopped a few feet away from him. Their eyes were level and unblinking. Tears made rivers down Ezra's cheeks and onto his shirt when he opened his arms and pulled her against him gently at first and then as tight as he could manage without harming the slight little girl.

"My baby...my baby," Ezra cooed over and over, unable to let go of the child, "Where have you been?" He rocked her against him, his eyes closed tightly as if holding in the flood of memories that washed over him at the touch of his daughter's arms hugging his neck.

"I've been all over, daddy. Papa Jude took me to so many neat places, but I just wanted to come home," she said into his chest, "I just wanted to come home to you."

At the mention of Jude's name, Ezra stopped rocking her and pulled her arms from his neck, leaning back to give her a second look. His eyes enflamed, and a cry choked in his throat at the sight of her pale skin and the slivers of fangs that she still tried to hide. He pulled his hands away from her cold skin as if it was burning him and stumbled to his feet.

"Ezra, don't be mad," Olivia said, pulling free of Nora and moving to her friend's side, taking her hand in her own, "It's not her fault."

Nora couldn't believe what she was seeing. Jude hadn't killed her. He'd turned her. All those years Ezra had spent missing her, grieving her, and she was traveling the world with Jude? Why would that monster keep her alive? There was no way that it was done as a kindness. Turning a child into a blood-sucking member of the undead could not be an act of love. There had to be an end game that he had been working towards. Now that Nora had given him his final death, there was a chance they would never know what that would have been. Regardless of the cruel game that Jude had been playing, Adalyn was able to stand in front of her father once again. She looked up at him with the mirrored irises of a vampire shining in the light.

"It's okay, daddy. Papa Jude is gone now. We can be a family again," she said, reaching for him and dropping her hand when he recoiled, "Please, Daddy. I'm sorry," she pleaded as cherry-colored tears pooled in the corners of her eyes.

"He did this to you? Jude made you...this?" Ezra spoke with poison on his tongue. His tearful joy had turned to disgust in an instant at the thought of his daughter becoming what he reviled most.

"Ezra, easy," Nora said, not wanting him to say something he would regret. She walked little by little to where they stood in a tense standoff, "The only thing that matters is that she's here. Ez, Adalyn has come back to you."

"Why? Why would he do this?" Ezra stared down at her, his face twitching from the onslaught of emotions. He held his hands up, away from her reach.

Adalyn looked to the floor; her shoulders slumped with the rejection, "He was lonely, daddy. He wanted a friend. I didn't want to go with him. I'm sorry. Please don't be mad at me."

Ezra looked to Nora, his eyes hollow and damp with tears, "What do I do? Why would...?" he looked to Adalyn, "How did this happen?" His arms dropped to his side with balled fists before he grabbed his head to steady himself against the raw grief that had scratched its way back to the surface. Adalyn said nothing and buried her head in Olivia's shoulder.

Nora started for the girls at the sight of the vampire's mouth nearing Olivia's neck before she realized the little girl was only seeking comfort in a hug from her friend. Ezra took breath after breath, each shorter than the last, as he became overwhelmed by what he knew to be reality and what he was happening right in front of him. Nora guided him to the chair, the furthest seat from the girls, and sat him down. He grabbed her arm and tugged her near to wrap her hand in his. She stood at his side, unsure of what should be done next. She made a silent plea that Gabriel would come for his visit sooner than later. A vampire would have more answers about what to do than she ever could.

"Olivia, is this the dancing girl you were talking about?" Nora speculated, keeping her voice low and stead. Ezra's hand tightened on hers.

"Yes! I told you she was real. Nobody ever believes me," Olivia moaned, "I always tell the truth! I needed your help, and you didn't believe me! Adalyn wasn't allowed to tell you guys she was here. The mean lady put her here right before mommy's coven did the charms so she couldn't get out!" Olivia put her arm around her friend and added, "She was trapped up there all by herself. Mommy took her dolls and everything. She's a good girl, Nora...*and* she knows how bad Sarah is. Tell them, Adalyn."

The spells and charms that Jenny had described were to keep vampires out. Even Gabriel was powerless against the strength of the coven. Nora hadn't considered that they could keep them in. The footsteps she had convinced herself were nothing more than creaking floors above her echoed in her memory. It was a trapped vampire, not an aging building that she had been falling asleep listening to.

Nora pushed on with her when Ezra retreated into himself, his face void of emotion from the stress of the revelation, "How did you get up there, Adalyn? Did Sarah put you up there? Is that why you think she's bad?" she asked, wishing she had listened to every last word that Olivia had said to her. If Sarah was against her, against all of them, they were in a perilous situation. High Priestess Maren told her not to trust anyone. All the while, she may have had a traitor in his own coven. She wondered if her words had been advice or a warning.

Olivia stomped her foot, making Nora jump, "Sarah knew she was up there and didn't want me to see her! She told mommy I was going up there so I would get in trouble. Sarah was gonna do bad things to me if I told you. I couldn't even tell Ezra, and he's her daddy. She's a bad lady who makes people sad on purpose, and I hate her!" Olivia wrapped her arms around Adalyn, who clung to her with sadness and fear.

Nora reached towards them and was promptly pulled back to Ezra's side. She perched on the side of the chair when she saw how he was shutting down and attempted to comfort him simultaneously with the girls. She wished Jenny would appear at the door to help her. This was too much to handle on her own.

"It's all right, Olivia. We'll make things right now. But I need to know how Adalyn got here. Was it Sarah?"

Adalyn dragged the back of her hand across her eyes, leaving faint streaks of bloody tears, and sniffled, "No, papa Jude's friend did, and Sarah's not as bad as Olivia thinks. She said she's going to be my new mama," she said with a shy smile to her father, "As soon as he gets rid of the gucky stuff they put in his blood, Auntie Quinn said she can make him like me, and we'll be together forever."

"*Who* said that?" Nora blurted. It had been unwise to assume that Quinn was finished with them, but harming a child was too far. Even for the heartless monster that she had become since being turned. Nora's stomach dropped at the mere mention of her aunt being involved.

"Auntie Quinn. That's Papa Jude's friend. But Sarah isn't bad cuz she said when daddy is like me, she's going to take care of both of us just like she's been taking care of me," Adalyn replied with an emerging cheer returning to her voice. She braved letting go of her friend and walked toward her father with trepidation. Reaching out, she took Ezra's free hand and entwined their fingers.

He did not recoil from his daughter. He just stared blankly, free of any emotion, at the ball of their two hands that now rested on his lap. He looked to his hand holding Nora's and back to his daughter's without a word. Nora was sure this had been the final nail in his mental undoing. Never before had she observed someone who had so wholly retreated. It left her feeling very alone and vulnerable, especially with the mention of Quinn.

She lowered herself to Adalyn's height, leaning on the arm of the chair and smiling her best open-hearted smile to the timid young vampire, "Quinn? It was Quinn who put you up there?"

"Yes. But Sarah brought me food. She always gives me little bags to drink every night, so I don't hurt," she answered, rubbing her belly, "If I don't eat, I feel like there's fire inside me," she added bashfully, giving a side glance to Ezra., "I'm sorry."

"It's ok, sweetie. There is nothing that you have to be sorry for," Nora's heart broke when she saw the sadness in her eyes when she looked at her broken father. Taking Ezra's jaw in her free hand, she gave him a shake, "Come on, Ez. You gotta stay with me right now," she begged and turned his head to face her, "I know this is a shock, but you need to listen to what she is saying. Quinn was here. He brought her here! Ezra, you need to snap out of this. Quinn knows about Adalyn!"

The mention of the murderous vampire's name brought Ezra's attention back into the room, his eyes blinking feverishly at the new information, "What? Quinn? Why would Quinn bring her here after all this time? How does she even know about her?" He looked down at his daughter, the pain still burning in his eyes, but he did not let go of her hand.

"I don't think she liked me very much," Adalyn said softly, "She didn't like when Papa Jude would give me attention. So, when Papa was gone, she said no one wanted me anymore. I haven't seen her since she left me up there. This used to be his house, you know."

"When was the last time you saw Quinn?" Nora asked evenly, willing her voice to stay calm and hoping to coax as much as she could from the frightened child, "When did she leave you here?"

"I don't know. She told me that Papa Jude was gone and not coming back," her pale lip began to tremble. Her words became shaky, "She said that my real daddy was going to come and get me. I had to sleep when the sun came up, and then I tried to leave up there to try and find you," she described, looking up under her damp lashes to her father, "but I couldn't get out of the door. I was really scared and hungry till Sarah came. I told her I wanted to find you. She said it would make you sad," her tears fell in heavy red drops when she watched her father silently cry as she spoke, "I guess Sarah was right."

Ezra let out a stiff, breathy cry of sorrow at the little girl's words and swept her up into his arms, burying his face in her long curls, "I'm not sad, baby. I'm not sad. I love you so much. I'm so sorry. I'm so, so sorry."

Nora stood, stepping back to witness the incredible moment, and Olivia ran to her side, wrapping her arms around her leg.

"I told you he would be happy to see you, Adalyn!" Olivia crowed, "No one ever listens to me."

"I think we should call Elijah," Nora said, wiping away a tear of her own that had fallen and patting her pockets for her phone, "and Jenny. Probably Gabriel. We need to call someone."

"No!" Adalyn shrieked and pulled herself up onto Ezra's lap, "Sarah said that man is going to take me away.

I'm not leaving daddy again! Don't call him! He's a bad man."

"Who's a bad man?" Nora asked, confused by her outburst, "No one's going to take you away, sweetie. We won't let them take you, I promise."

"Sarah said Elijah won't let me stay with Daddy because I'm too young to be what Jude made me. She said he would take me away and hurt me," Adalyn exclaimed, eyes wild with fear.

Nora kneeled back down to her, 'No, it's okay. He's not a bad man. I know him; it's going to be all right," Nora tried to console her, "He can help us."

Adalyn's loveable face curled into a sneer in a flash, "I don't believe you. Sarah said you're the one who took Papa Jude away from me, and you would take daddy, too."

"I..." Nora looked at Ezra, fearful of the anger on her face. It had been Nora who had staked Jude to save Ezra's life. She could not fathom keeping Ezra from her daughter and would never allow it to happen again. Sarah had planted a whole lot of lies in that child's head and heart. It was not a crush she had on Ezra; Sarah was obsessed.

Olivia put a hand on her friend's shoulder, a solemn look overtaking her young face, "Adalyn, I told you it's not true. Sarah tells lies. You know she does. She's the one that wanted to keep you locked up there. Nora would have come get you if I was allowed to tell her.

Sarah is bad!" Olivia insisted, standing in front of Nora protectively, "Nora is good, Adalyn."

They all jumped at the sound of alarm buzzing, announcing sunset. If they survived the night, Nora promised herself that they would replace the screaming bell of the alarm with something less heart-stopping. She spotted her cell phone on the coffee table and reached for it quickly. Her hands scanned the contacts, wondering whom she should call first.

Her finger hovered over Jenny's name when a shrill whistle called out from someone on the street below. Nora closed the space between herself and the window in a few fast paces. She started to open the window to get a better look when the visitor stepped back further from the building, onto the street, and into sight.

Quinn sneered up at her under the pale yellow glow of the streetlight before she launched into the air, stopping at her window, eye to eye with Nora.

"Hiya, Squirt. Did you get my gift?"

CHAPTER FIFTEEN

Quinn was a hair's thickness from the window as she rapped her fingers on the glass and smiled at her niece with a viper's grin when she stumbled back, barely staying on her feet. Her eyes no longer had any signs of the loving woman Nora had initially sought out in Aumbry Valley. The heat that burned in her reflective irises was pure hatred. She had plans of mass destruction yet made a point to start with Nora. There was no way around the confrontation that hovered outside the window in the freshly darkened sky. Quinn was there to finish things one way or another. Nora moved the young girls behind her, wishing more than anything that she hadn't volunteered to spend the afternoon with Olivia so she would have been downstairs and out of harm's way.

Quinn looked from person to person, predatory and hungry, "Why don't you make this easy and invite me in, Nora? I have far more important things than you to get to, but somehow, you're like a vein stuck between my teeth after a good meal. You're a nagging bother that I just can't ignore," Quinn whined, pressing her nose to the glass, "Just invite me in, Squirt," she narrowed her eyes when Nora didn't respond to her attempted influence, "So, you do still have that disgusting fae blood swirling around in you, huh?"

Knowing that, at least at the moment, she had enough of the serum left to keep Quinn out of her head gave Nora a little more courage, and she widened her stance, standing defiantly against her, "That's right! You can't make me, Quinn. You're stuck out there."

Ezra moved to her side in solidarity, tucking the two small girls behind him as well as an added layer of protection when Quinn turned her attention their way. She gave Adalyn a wave and a poorly feigned smile. Nora could feel the anger radiating from him before he even spoke, "There's no way you're getting in here, Quinn. Just go. There are a lot of people watching this place, and you're living on minutes out there."

"Oh, you mean the two morons who they have looking out for you? They're going to come up here and take care of me?" Quinn asked with a laugh. She dragged her fingernail down the glass of the window pane, a sharp cut squealing along down to the bottom. Nora was glad when the glass didn't give way, "What if I told you that they weren't even there?" she tittered, "Face it, you don't matter to them anymore. None of you do," she placed her palms on the glass, "and now that they know what I have? You think they'd have the balls to challenge me? Do you think you can do anything, big guy? I have all the power, and it's surging through my veins like a God. You're a pathetic little man who hides away like a coward."

Nora stepped slowly back towards the table, hoping to get her phone while Quinn was focused on Ezra and the girls.

"I'm not going to take the bait, Quinn. Say whatever you want. It doesn't matter. The coven has made sure that you can't get in here. You need to leave. We don't want any part of what you're doing," Ezra said firmly. Nora was thankful that he was keeping his cool. They just needed to keep everyone away from the window until they could signal for help.

"I could not care less about what you want, coward," her eyes flicked to Nora and the phone in her shaking hand, "And who exactly are you going to call, Nora? Vamp-busters?" she let out a howling, deranged laugh that chilled Nora to the bone, "You're on your own, Squirt, and I promise you that tonight is going to be your last night on earth. I promise you all that," her nail squealed down along the window, the scratch getting more visible.

"I didn't ask for any of this, Quinn. I just wanted my best friend back. If I could go back in time and never come here, you can bet your ass I would never have come within a hundred miles of this cursed town. Please, leave us alone," Nora sputtered, doing her best not to let the tears flow. She would not let Quinn have the satisfaction.

"Oh, poor little Nora-bird," Quinn spat the words and slammed a fist on the window, "Do you know why I left? Do you know why I needed to escape?" her eyes glowed with every word she shot to her, "I spent my life with you under my heel, being told by my *own* father to look after you. Keep Nora safe. Cheer Nora up. Nora, Nora, fucking Nora! All the while, I was never good enough for him. He loved you, didn't he, Nora? Always with a kind word and a push in the right direction. What did he do for me? I was the worthless one, the one who was wasting her life—wandering around from place to place with abandon. He couldn't see that I was so desperately trying to find my way. I didn't have anyone looking out for me! I was doing it all on my own, all the while watching you being given all the help you needed. Just because your parents knew what a waste of skin they had made," she pushed on, louder when Nora shook her head, trying to shut out the hate-filled words, "He liked what he saw in you because it was himself. You were just like him, and the selfish prick could only love someone that he saw his favorite person in," she pressed her lips tightly, holding in the emotions that wanted to escape before the anger could retake hold, "I finally found somewhere that I mattered to, somewhere where I was the one that was important. Someone that loved me! And you took it all away from me, just like you always did! Well, not anymore, Squirt. You're done."

Nora couldn't believe the words she was hurling at her. The pain in her aunt's eyes was something she had never seen, even on the night that she had lost Jude. Nora had never considered that Quinn was anything but happy. As a child, she idolized her cool, free-spirited hero, never seeing that she was harboring a pain so deep that she was willing to die to be rid of it. The grandfather that Nora remembered never had a cruel word to say about anyone but his son, Nora's father. Looking back, she realized that if he could be hateful of one child, he could have been to the other. He could have been what created the cold man who was so hard-hearted toward Nora. If that was possible, it wasn't impossible to think he had planted the same broken seeds of cruelty in his daughter. It was hard to picture him breaking Quinn down to what she now was, but the proof was right in front of her eyes.

Nora wanted to apologize for not knowing. She wanted to hug her tightly and squeeze all of the darkness from her unbeating heart, "Why didn't you tell me all of this before?"

"Oh, fragile Nora with the mean old parents who gave her everything she wanted couldn't be bothered with anything. I couldn't burden you with my feelings. My father always told me to be like the parent my useless brother wasn't. Just like my father never was for me."

Nora took a few steps towards her, stopping herself when she remembered the risk, "I'm so sorry, Quinn. I honestly didn't know you were feeling this way. I am so, so sorry, but hurting other people isn't going to take your pain away. You have to know that! You need to stop all of this and turn yourself in. It's not too late to fix all of what's happened."

Quinn's eyes widened, and she dragged her nail sharply down the glass, this time from right to left, leaving an etching of a cross, "It's not, is it? Want to tell that to Jude? That it's not too late? You saw to it that there was no turning back!" she pressed her palm to the glass. It started to vibrate with her touch, "I'm not looking to get rid of my pain, bitch. I'm looking to get rid of a problem. You."

"Auntie Quinn, please don't get angry. You're scaring my friend," Adalyn said, slipping from behind Ezra.

Quinn softened her expression, smiling at the girl who bravely stood in front of the window, "Adalyn, sweetheart, why don't you bring your little friend over here so I can meet her properly?"

Ezra put a protective arm around Olivia, "No, Quinn. Leave her out of this."

"Come here, cutie-pie. It's okay. I'm sorry I shouted. Come let me have a look at you," Quinn said smoothly, trying to lock eyes with the petrified little girl who knew enough to keep her eyes to the floor.

Nora moved over to add another layer between them, "Quinn, I mean it. Leave her alone."

Quinn ignored her and pushed on with the little vampire," Adalyn, it's all right. Just ask her to come over here to meet me. I'd like to apologize for scaring her. Just like I showed you, sweetheart. Always look someone in the eye when you talk to them. Look her in the eye and tell her to come over and meet me, sweetheart."

Nora knew what she was telling Adalyn to do and kept a protective arm outstretched to keep the tiny vampire from being able to influence Olivia. Adalyn looked between Quinn and the three. There was a connection to Quinn that left her confused as to whom she should listen to.

Adalyn looked up sadly at her father, "Daddy, she's come here so we can be a family again. Let her come in, please," she pleaded, "She won't hurt you. She promised me that she wouldn't hurt you."

Ezra reached for her and took her hand, pulling her back from the window, "No, Adalyn. She is a bad person, and she *will* hurt us," Ezra said, shifting Olivia more directly behind him, "You need to believe Daddy."

"I told you, didn't I, Adalyn? That mean lady doesn't want you to have your daddy. Just like she took Papa Jude from us," Quinn pushed, "Everything I've told you is true, sweetheart. Your Daddy wants to be with Nora and your little friend. They're the ones keeping you from your daddy."

Olivia slipped out from behind the protection of Ezra and rushed toward the window, "No! You're the bad lady! Nora is good!" she shouted, "Get out of here before I get my friends to take care of you!"

Quinn grinned wickedly at the close proximity of the angry little mortal and slid down the window to get a better lock on her eyes, "Why don't you invite me in, and we can sort all of this out, little one? You want to invite me in."

"Don't look in her eyes, Olivia!" Nora screamed, grabbing the girl and spinning her away from the threat, "What kind of person uses children like that? You're a fucking monster now, Quinn. Get the hell out of here!"

Quinn stilled in place, a deathly stare locked on her niece, "What I am is free, Nora. I'm not anchored to anyone or any place, and I'm more powerful than you could ever imagine," she slid her hand into the pocket of her jacket to pull out a smooth glass bottle that was the size and shape of a pear. The crimson liquid inside glowed in the moonlight when she sloshed it around in front of her before she popped off the glass stopper and took a sip. She smiled with the blood still staining her teeth when she replaced the cap and tucked it back into her jacket. Her eyes blazed a red heat that slowly filled the entire surface of her eyes. Her body quivered with the pleasure the blood was bringing her, "The maker is in me now, Nora. There is no one more fierce than I am."

"Says the bitch who can't even get into an old building," Ezra shouted, pulling the girls back into the room.

Quinn started to erupt with anger for only a moment. She swallowed the outburst and calmly placed her finger on the glass, pointing it to him, the glass slowly cracking under her pressure. Nora held her breath as the glass held its place, "I was going to go along with the little brat and her lovestruck witch friend and let you live, *you dumb fuck*, but now I think I may snap you like a twig just to hear the crack."

Adalyn grabbed Ezra's hand, moving him quickly back with a strength that a five-year-old should not possess, "Auntie Quinn! Don't talk to my daddy like that!"

"Will you stop whining for five damn minutes?" Quinn barked at her, "I swear, I have no idea why Jude kept you around, you snot-nosed little brat!"

"I told you she's bad, Adalyn!" Olivia yelled, "She wants to hurt all of us. She's bad, just like Sarah."

Nora wished she had the stake that she kept on her dresser. It was close enough to see, but she didn't want to leave Olivia's side. She started to try to tug her along, inching toward her bedroom. With the power of the maker's blood rushing through her, Quinn may be strong enough to bypass the coven's charms. If she breached the building, there was no way that they would stand a chance against her. She wanted to have every weapon she could find to protect the children. Hopefully, she could buy enough time to get them out and to safety before Quinn finally got her ultimate revenge. It was time to make peace with what may happen to her. There was no way it would go down without a fight, and she would do whatever she needed to save the innocent girls who had already been through more than they could ever deserve. Ezra saw she was going for the stake and felt the side pocket of his pants, giving Nora a nod. Two stakes would be better than none, and Nora prayed that Ezra's new training would help them out. Time was up, and no one was appearing to help.

"Where are you going, Squirt? Going to hide away in your room, like you always have?" Quinn laughed cruelly, "Gonna let a little girl and her daddy do all the work?"

The words spurred Nora on, and she moved confidently to grab the stake and hold it out to her, keeping Olivia back with her other hand, "Quinn, I don't know why you've been letting me live rent-free in your head all these years, and I have no idea how to fix any of this, but I'm begging you. Leave these kids alone. Your fight is with me. This is not their fault."

"Then come outside, tough girl. You're the one hiding in there with them. Leave them in your shitty apartment and come and face me. Let's get this over with," Quinn looked up and down the silent street, pleasure creeping across her lips.

Nora stepped slowly over to Ezra and shifted Olivia behind him with Adalyn. She gave him a weak smile that was drawn with defeat. It was time for it to end one way or another, and there did not seem to be any cavalry to the rescue this time. It was up to her to take a stand.

Ezra grabbed her hand and gripped it tightly, "No, Nora. No fucking way are you going out there!"

Nora wriggled free, shaking her head at his protest, "She's right, Ez. This doesn't involve any of you. This is my fault."

He reached for her again, "The hell it is! Nora, It's not your fault she's a psychopath drunk on power. Please, Nora. Someone will come soon. You don't have to do this," Ezra pleaded, looking from the girls to her.

Nora knew he was trying to figure out how to protect them all at once, and they both knew that it was impossible. If she went down, he would stay with the girls. He would keep them safe. She started for the door, attempting to block Ezra's pleas to remain as she clicked away at the locks and put her hand on the doorknob.

"Norma! Please don't go! Don't leave us. We need you," Olivia cried out, stopping Nora, "We have to stick together. Mommy says that's what families do!"

Nora looked to the little girl whose tears streamed down her reddened cheeks, her little shoulders shaking with sobs. Adalyn looked up at her dad with confused terror; tiny drips of blood tears fell from her lashes. Ezra stared back at Nora, shaking his head slowly, his eyes desperate.

The pain in their eyes opened her heart to what her own truth had become. The woman hovering outside the building was not her family. Ezra was. Olivia and Jenny were. In a way, Adalyn now was. Her family was under that roof, and she would not leave them to fight on their own. She knew she was going out there to be slaughtered, exhausted by the months of fear, confinement, and unknowing that had filled her life day after day. She was going out there to give up, not to fight. Quinn would find a way to destroy them all one way or another. Olivia was right. Families stuck together, and that's exactly what they would do. They would hold down the fort until the end. Together.

Nora released the door handle and started to return to where they stood when the door pushed open behind her. Quinn let out a celebratory whoop and knocked her knuckles to the glass when she saw who had arrived.

Sarah stood on the threshold, her sad eyes on Ezra, "I'm so sorry, but it has to be done," she apologized before turning to the window, "Come in, Quinn."

The windowpane exploded in tiny, skin-ripping shards across the room when Quinn launched her fist through, and she was nose-to-nose with Nora before anyone could process what had happened. Quinn's right hand's long, cold fingers snaked across Nora's throat while her other hand effortlessly crushed the stake that Nora held into sawdust. The pain of her bones crushing against the slivered wood made Nora's face twist and contort, unable to scream under Quinn's grip.

Quinn released her hand to pluck up a piece of the silver that had broken away from the crushed stake. She traced it down Nora's cheek to scratch out a trickle of warm blood before she leaned in closer to inhale the scent of the fresh wound. Her nose twitched, and she grimaced at the smell of the remaining fae blood. Taking in the scent deeper, her eyes flickered with mischievous malice, "Oh, this is going to be fun."

CHAPTER SIXTEEN

Ezra grabbed onto his daughter's arm when she tried to run to Nora, her eyes dilated with hunger from the fresh trickle of blood, "Adalyn, no stay back!" He fiercely held her until she was able to get control of herself and step behind her father, clinging desperately to his shirt to keep herself back from her desire to feed, "Sarah, what the hell is going on? Why would you invite that bitch in here?" he bellowed across the apartment. Sarah did not acknowledge him or the girls and kept her attention on Nora and Quinn, "Sarah, answer me! Why would you help her?"

Muttering an incantation under her breath, Sarah became more insistent with her words when Nora's cries increased. The unseeable spiders started to consume her face as they did before, filling her mouth and throat, which were already being choked of breath. Quinn held her hands away from swatting them with the fist that was not wrapped around Nora's neck. Not being able to scratch at the invisible attackers deepened the torture. Her body arched and twisted, trying to free herself; her head was immovable under Quinn's grip. The pounding of her heels against the floor echoed along with the screams of the little girls as they watched.

Ezra shuffled them into the limited safety of the farthest corner and started for Nora before turning back to the girls. It was an impossible choice to make. He screamed at Sarah to stop, unable to move or decide whom to help first.

"Stop it!" the girls yelled in unison to the women holding Nora at their whim. They cowered in each other's arms, tucking themselves against the wall. Covering their eyes, they rocked back and forth in an attempt to soothe their terror. Sarah and Quinn made no notice of their presence and carried on with their barrage of cruelty. Nora's vision faded into the watery tears that blurred the room around her. The girls' screams were almost more painful than the blinding eruption of agony that filled her head when Quinn slammed it back against the hardwood floor.

Sarah's voice rose louder, pushing the unintelligible words into action. Quinn roared with devious laughter at Nora's obvious pain, her fear feeding her happiness. Nora tried to plead with her to apologize for whatever it was that pushed Sarah to act with such cruelty. She could only scream in desperation when she felt the spiders burrowing into her skin.

"Sarah, you're better than this. Please. Let her go," Ezra begged, "You need to stop this!"

Sarah abruptly silenced the chant and gave him a look of remorse, "What else can I do, Ezra? I've done everything to try to make you happy! I even took care of your daughter after Quinn dumped her here. No matter what I do, you only care about her!" Sarah spat the words in Nora's direction, "What's so special about her?"

Nora tried to process Sarah's words as the tiny spiders disappeared from her face, a fleeting moment of relief before Quinn doubled down on her grip. Stars lit up in her vision, a warning of inevitable unconsciousness.

Sarah had gone behind the coven's back, sided with Quinn, and kept Adalyn a secret all because of unrequited feelings for Ezra. Nora could not comprehend that Sarah could be so vindictive. She was never standing in the way of the two being together, and Adalyn had surely suffered enough. Sarah had to have lost her mind if she thought any of her evil and twisted plans would lead to Ezra choosing to be with her.

Quinn's constant laughter sounded miles away. Focusing on her face, the dark, hate-filled eyes stared back at her with twisted amusement. Her fangs were still stained with the maker's blood she had downed from the small bottle.

Sarah stepped away from them and toward Ezra, "I'm sorry. I didn't know what else to do. I know we're supposed to be together. It's not only my heart that's telling me. The tarot told me the same thing. We're destined to be together, Ezra. I know it, and you know it," she spoke slowly, moving closer, "We can be a family now. You, me, and Adalyn. We're meant to be."

"Sarah, are you insane? Why would I feel anything but hatred for you now that I see who you really are?" Ezra countered, "And you think I will let you anywhere near my daughter? You're fucking nuts! Seriously, stop this before it's too late," he demanded, holding his arm out to keep her from getting any closer to the girls.

Nora's stomach lurched when Quinn rose to her feet, lifting Nora by her throat with ease and then throwing her to the ground. She crumpled in a heap at her feet, gulping in air as deeply as her aching lungs would allow. Trying to pull herself away, a sharp shock of pain in the base of her neck stopped her in place. Quinn had done more damage than choking. Nora worried that if she moved another inch, she would worsen what could become a broken neck. She risked moving her legs, glad to see they would even though they were weak from Quinn's attack. If any fae blood was left in her system, she hoped it would be enough to help her heal.

Quinn gave Nora's back a kick, causing her to howl in agony, and stepped over her, "Can you take your little romance outside, witch? You're ruining my fun."

Sarah's chest rose and fell with quick, anxious breaths, "You said you would help me, Quinn! You said you would..." she trailed off with a quiet, defeated sob and turned her sad eyes to Ezra.

Footfalls pounded up the stairs, getting closer quickly. Nora prayed it was someone, anyone, who could help them.

"What the hell is going on?" Jenny breathlessly shouted as she ran in and stopped short when she saw the gathering, "Oh shit," she sputtered and stared at Quinn, who was still standing over Nora, "How did she...oh shit!" she swore louder when she saw her daughter cowering in the corner and moved in a flash to gather her in her arms. She stood beside Adalyn, only glancing at her before turning back to the nightmarish scene playing out in her building, "What is going on? What do you want?"

"What do I want?" Quinn sneered, "Oh, girl. That is a long list," she gave Nora another kick, "At the moment, it's to watch the life extinguish from this little bitch's eyes and then, oh, I don't know, probably total world domination," her lips drew back to reveal the fanged grin of a predator, "As for the naughty little *witch* over there, she wants me to turn that fine piece of meat over there, so he'll forever be stuck in these walls with his little brat spawn. I guess if you can't win the man, you trap the man. Romance, right? Now that I'm getting a better look at him, I might just keep him for myself. "

Sarah's eyes widened, and her mouth opened and closed before she could speak, "Quinn! You promised!"

"I know, I do that a lot," she cackled and reached down to grab Nora when she tried and failed to drag herself closer to the door, "Not so fast." She held her up like a weightless rag doll and shook a finger in her face, "Tsk, tsk, tsk, Squirt. You're not leaving the party when you're the guest of honor," she tossed her again, causing a shock of pain through Nora's body that felt like a lightning strike. Bile burned up from her gut, and she heaved. Every tiny movement felt as if a nail was being hammered into her neck. Quinn squatted down to meet her eyes, "Now do I want him to watch you die, or would it be more fun for you to watch him getting ripped to pieces?"

"Quinn! We had a deal," Sarah objected. She started towards Ezra and stopped, hanging her head in shame when she saw the look of revulsion he gave her. He picked up Adalyn and stood shoulder-to-shoulder with Jenny.

"Sarah, this can't be true!" Jenny gawked at her with disbelief, "Is that why you suggested the spell? You didn't want to help anyone. You just wanted to...what? Make Ezra some sort of love slave?"

"It's not like that! Jenny, you know me. The charms were to keep you safe. To keep everyone safe. I didn't know she was up there until after, and then the idea to keep Ezra just," she swallowed back the whimper that tried to escape, "Please believe me."

"Believe you? You brought her into my home, into Olivia's home, and I'm supposed to believe that you care about keeping us safe? And what do you mean you didn't know she was up there? Quinn has been hiding in this building the whole time?" Jenny pulled her daughter closer and turned to see Ezra's reaction to Sarah's confession. She jumped away from him when her eyes took in the child in his arm, settling on her pale skin and tiny fangs, "Who is that? Jesus, Quinn, did you do this?" she stuttered.

"Oh, come on. No, even I wouldn't turn a child," Quinn answered, slowly lifting Nora again until her toes were barely touching the floor, "That was Jude's little plaything," she watched Nora as if she were a bored, twisted child pulling the legs from an insect.

"Let her down!" Ezra cried out.

Nora could feel her mind and body giving in to the repeated abuse at Quinn's hand. The room spun away with each assault, and she would try to focus on anyone or anything but Quinn when her eyes would allow, "Let them go," she mouthed with a weak breath, "Please, let them go."

"What's that?" Quinn asked, holding Nora's head closer to hear her strangled voice, "Let them go? Ha! That's not going to happen," Quinn spat. She pulled the glass bottle from her pocket with her free hand, uncorking it with one of her razor-sharp fangs, and giggled as she pressed the edge to Nora's gaping mouth. A tiny drop glistened on her lip, "I wonder how much of that dirty fae blood is left in you, huh? Not enough to fix your pathetic little broken body, huh?" she put her lips to Nora's ear to hiss, "Just a little sip will tell me. If there's as much as I can smell on your rancid breath, there's enough to let me watch you burn from the inside out. This stuff is insane. So fun."

Nora tried to keep the drop of blood that spread on her lip from entering her mouth. She knew exactly what would happen if it mixed with any fae blood. Elijah had been clear about that. Nora tried to focus on Ezra. He had to get away from that bottle. If Quinn gave any amount to him, he would surely die. The fae blood the bureau had given him was still fresh in his system. She squinted, willing herself to stay conscious, and wished she could scream for him to leave. His pained eyes stared helplessly back at her when she tried to mouth, I'm sorry. Her heart twisted in ripping knots at the sight of the two young girls recoiling away from the horror they were witnessing. It was fine if Quinn wanted her dead. The cold numbness that was creeping over her body told her to make peace with that. If she did manage to escape, it was a future of constant war with the person who was once her best friend—someone whom she never wanted to be on opposite sides from the beginning. If fate had brought her to this point, fate could decide what would happen next. The will to live was weakening as quickly as the strength of her body. The only thing pressing her to stay was the thought of anything happening to Ezra. That would haunt her beyond her own grave. After all that he had been through, he finally had his daughter back. No matter what Adalyn now was, she was back in his life. There was no way that his hatred of vampires would extend to his own flesh and blood. He was a good man who didn't deserve any of the pain he had been drowning in.

Quinn's grip tightened and loosened for a flash, just enough to keep Nora conscious. She was playing with her, drawing out the inevitable ending, and she loved every minute of it. Nora let her body go limp. The streak of pain that shot down her spine from the weight of her own body caused an explosion of adrenaline within her and the room came into focus as if she had just surfaced from icy waters.

Quinn noticed Nora's attention on Ezra and turned her broken body towards him with a flick of her wrist, "You think your little vampire hunter over there is going to help you? You think he's got what it takes to take me on with the amount of maker's blood coursing through me?" Quinn snorted, "Didn't he need *you* to save him last time we met? From the smell of him, one little drop of this and he's gone."

"No! Quinn, you can't," Sarah begged, "You can't hurt him!"

"I can do whatever I want! I don't owe any of you anything. I get to decide who lives and who dies now, and I don't see why any of you should get to live. Jude didn't get to," Quinn held up the bottle, "I'm the one in charge now."

The bottle touched Nora's lips once more. The cold, copper taste of blood trickled on her tongue. She spat it out as best she could with Quinn's hand still snaked around her neck, just loose enough for it to trickle down her throat.

"You willfully let them put the disgusting blood of fairies in you, and you dare spit back the sacred blood of the maker?" Quinn released her, letting her collapse in a pile at her feet, "How dare you? You never did appreciate a damn thing, did you? You're a spoiled little bitch, Nora!"

She grabbed Nora by the foot and spun her across the floor, into the wall, with a strength none of them had ever seen. In an instant, Sarah jumped towards the door and was down the stairs, running from the disaster she had facilitated. Before Nora could catch her breath, Quinn was straddling her chest. The crimson-stained bottle was tipped to her lips again.

"Quinn, please..." Nora pleaded with a broken and hoarse voice, "Just let them go. Please."

Quinn held up the bottle, examining the remaining contents, "I'm not sure what I'll do with them, Squirt. I don't have a lot of this left," she leaned in close, her lips wet on Nora's cheek, "I have a lot more stored away for me, but the rest of this is for you. You're going to burn for what you did."

Quinn shoved the bottle into Nora's mouth, pressing it through her tightly closed lips. She used every last bit of energy left in her body to push back and gagged as the blood pooled in her throat before it choked its way down. The burn started immediately, racing like flames down into her stomach and spreading through her veins like the wind to a blaze. Her body began to contort against the painful attack within. Turning her head to the side, her eyes locked on Ezra. Jenny desperately tried to hold him back with the girls, the edge of his shirt ripping as she struggled to hold on.

"No! No, no, no! Please god! No!" he screamed, tears wetting his agonized face.

The pain pulled Nora's body into a ball, sweat covering her body. Her fingers curled tightly into fists that she held close to her chest as she convulsed violently. Her breath came in short, helpless gasps as her vision fogged into a liquid red haze. Blinking, she tried to see through, staring up at the ceiling, knowing that it would be the last thing she would ever see. She was ready for the pain to stop, even if it meant she had to let go. The sounds around her softened as a ringing in her ears took over, her heart pounding loudly and slower with each beat. Everything around her started to slow. A small feather floated down towards her, and her mind found peace in the slow drift. Another larger black feather appeared, followed by another. Guilt replaced peace when Gail's face appeared in her mind. If it were her, the frail, old woman would have no power over Quinn with the power of the blood she held. No matter what a peri could do, Nora doubted she could take on Quinn. She would become another victim of having the bad luck of crossing paths with Nora.

A flash of black feathers whooshed over top of her and then another. Wings that were much larger and darker than Gail's rustled over her and into the room. The tall man they belonged to headed straight for Quinn, closing the space between them faster than her eyes could follow. Grabbing her by the throat in the same way that she had just held Nora, he held her up as far as his arm would reach. Turning to Nora, she caught sight of the man's rage-filled face.

Norman.

He growled at Quinn angrily, and his massive wings stretched out to his sides when he let out a piercing war cry.

The last thing Nora heard before the world went black was the distinct sharp crack of Quinn's neck breaking.

CHAPTER SEVENTEEN

V

Nora didn't know how long she had been out before becoming aware of the space around her again. It began with the pain that burned through her veins, still raging within her, trying to destroy her every cell one by one. She fought against what she could only believe was the death of her body, wanting to stretch against the tight pull in her muscles and scream, but she was left immobile and silent, trapped within a body that would not respond to the invasion of toxic blood. Slowly, the pain lessened to a level of a constant yet manageable boil, and she was able to hear voices muffled around her.

"Now is not the time to worry about that, Gabriel," Elijah's voice briefly broke through the constant hum in Nora's ears. He sounded far too loud, yet he wasn't shouting. Everything sounded too loud, and Nora's head thumped with the effort of breaking up and recognizing each sound.

Eventually, the pain attempting to rip her body apart was replaced by a slow, deep heat that simmered just under her skin. The passing of time was impossible to track. Her eyes refused to open, and her mind refused to sleep. The constant noise around her was indecipherable, and she lay paralyzed and confused. The thought of what had happened to her left her with more questions than answers.

If she was dead, why could she hear Elijah's voice? If she was amongst demons in the afterlife, she had a good idea of where she was. Nora could not think of anything she had done in life that would send her down there. Could it be that taking Jude's life to spare Ezra's came at the cost of her soul? Unless it was the maker's blood that was enough to damn her for eternity.

There were feathers.

Why were there feathers? She wondered if she had been in the presence of an angel when she remembered feathers as black as onyx. As black as a stone that she pushed to remember. The obsidian stone. It was black, not green. Why did she think it was green? She could see the photo she had been looking at. Obsidian stones were black.

Sarah. It was Sarah that had given her the green stone. Memories of being attacked started to drift in one piece at a time. The more she became aware of what had happened, the more she worried about what had become of the others. She could see Ezra's tortured eyes, the terror in Olivia's.

Who else had been there?

The crack of a bone breaking snapped over and over in her head until she was sure she would go mad. The feathers returned to her waking dream, drifting in and dulling the sound. Soft and black, they felt as if they were enveloping her. Norman's feathers! The memory of her shy, shut-in neighbor rushing in and saving her life filled her with light.

Was he an angel?

Whatever he was, she was sure that he had been the end of Quinn. The look in his eye had been one of vengeance. Nora hoped that it was only Quinn that he had gone after.

Her own voice screamed in her head, trapped along with the rest of her when her ears would pick up conversations that were happening around her, desperate for someone to hear her. She could pick out separate voices more and more, and she welcomed the company even if she could not clearly understand the words they spoke. Most she did not recognize. Usually, it was Gabriel and Elijah arguing in hushed tones that sounded as if someone had turned up the volume within them. One voice that called out to her gave her hope and horror all at once. Jenny was by her side. Either Nora had been alive all along, or Jenny was dead as well. The thought of Olivia growing up without her mother was far more distressing than the residual pain she had felt from the maker's blood.

Nora's racing thoughts froze when she felt Jenny take her hand. She could feel her! She could feel something other than pain and she willed her fingertips to twitch up and then her toes. Sensations rushed over every delicate nerve ending of her body, overwhelming her. Her heavy eyelids fluttered open, fighting against the far too-bright room. She could feel the slightest movement of air against her skin and the warmth of the light that sat on a table beside her. The room spun around her, causing her stomach to wretch, and she clamped her eyes closed when she swallowed the saliva that pooled in her mouth, readying her throat to vomit. Once she was able to settle the queasiness, she took in the sensations of all of her senses returning to her.

She wasn't dead.

She couldn't believe that she had survived the attack from Quinn. There was no other outcome that she could imagine in the moment, and she was on the other side of the fight. She was alive, and so was Jenny. The murmur of voices in the room sounded far away and too loud all at once. A ripple of nausea had her clutching her stomach. She peered at the space around her, what she could see through the blinding light. She could see nothing more than a few inches in front of her. Unable to move her head, she turned her eyes as far as she could to the small side lamp that was bright enough to make her clamp her eyelids shut again. She couldn't understand how a light of that size could have such an effect.

"Nora, can you hear me?" Elijah asked, his voice echoing as if in a dream.

She tried to answer, even to nod her head, but the heat that boiled under her skin held steady and held her down, unable to move. Her eyes refused to open again.

"There has to be someone who knows what to do. We can't leave her suffering like this forever," Gabriel's voice filled the room. His voice had an edge of compassion that she had never heard from the flippant vampire.

"This would be more your area of expertise, Gabriel. You tell me," Elijah replied.

The room spun quickly as she felt her body falling into a dark abyss that swallowed her whole. She tried to call out for help, not wanting the darkness to return. The burning pain slipped away along with the sounds of the room until she was unaware of her own existence once more. She lived in this cycle of life and death that felt never-ending for days. Only catching small quips of conversation, never being able to take part. The pain would return with the hope of life and then gratefully being taken away along with all that she was—days on end of all or nothing.

A voice that she didn't recognize pulled her from the nothingness, "It's still touch and go right now," a woman said, "Damn it, how was she able to get her hands on that blood. There had to be more involved than just that little love-sick witch."

"Everyone is being looked at for this. It is indeed unprecedented," Elijah said stiffly.

"If that virtue hadn't arrived in time, we would be dealing with an all-out war on all levels. How was an angel living in this valley, and you had no idea," the unknown woman admonished.

"I do admit to my failures throughout the bureau, ma'am. I freely admit that. However, you and I know that this goes deeper than my bureau and even The Firm as a whole," Elijah retorted, his polite tone tense with impatience.

Nora strained to hear more as the darkness started to swallow her again, even as she fought against it. This time it was not a dreamless death. Norman's face appeared and dissipated over and over in her mind, feathers swirling around his intense eyes.

An angel had been in the valley. *Was Norman an angel?* The thought spiraled until she was swallowed once more into the nothingness.

When she next felt pulled to the surface of awareness, the searing pain across her flesh was nearly gone. The pressure in her head was left only as a dull ache, and she had the strength to twitch a few more fingers. The voices in the room were more clearly understood.

"If the fae blood had been completely out of her system, she would have transitioned by now. If some had remained, she should have expired instantly," a woman's voice advised whoever was in the room.

The voices were of a tolerable level, and the vibration to each word that made her eardrums feel as if they would burst was gone. Nora wanted nothing more than to ask them what was happening to her, and she tried to drag her eyes open, silently screaming when they remained sealed. The more the pain lessened, the more she felt trapped in her body, unable to call out or even see who surrounded her. A warmth caressed her lips, and she felt them part. A smooth liquid dripped into her mouth and slid down her throat. The taste exploded against her tongue, more delicious than anything she had ever experienced. Her body relaxed into the ecstasy that overcame her until it hit her stomach. Starting from a pinprick of pain, it quickly erupted into every cell in her body. The agony returned. Nora could not understand why they were continuing to torment her. It had to be the maker's blood again breaking apart her body. Her back lurched and stiffened against the internal intrusion until she gratefully fell back into the dark abyss. It felt as if it only lasted for a blink of an eye before she was returned to her suffering body.

"If she's held on this long, we owe it to her to see this through, no matter what the council says," Elijah's voice said through her haze.

"We can't just let her suffer like this," Ezra's shaking voice joined the conversation.

He was alive! Nora tried to call out his name. Her dry mouth refused to open. Using all of the effort that she could muster, she pushed her tongue forward, trying to wet her lips. A sharp pinch sliced into the flesh, followed by a small drop of metallic moisture. She tried again and had the same result. Lifting her tongue as best as she could manage, she felt the cause. Needle-sharp fangs had replaced her canine teeth. A soft moan of fear vibrated in her chest. She pushed herself to feel them again. She tried to lift her hands to her mouth and found her body was still paralyzed under the unseen weight holding her down.

"Nora! Nora, can you hear me?" Ezra called out to her. She felt his warm hand cover hers.

Centering all of the energy that she could, she managed one slight nod of her head before exhaustion pulled her under again.

This time, the empty darkness of unconsciousness broke away into a feeling of floating outside her body and the ability to move it all at once. Falling back through a seemingly bottomless void, a light began to glow below her, brighter and brighter, until she landed softly, wrapped in the soft illumination. Her hands felt around at the blanket she was spread across, grateful to be able to move her limbs. She recognized that she was on a bed. She was able to sit up in a room that had been swallowed in fog, making it hard to decipher what was around her. The nightside table beside her held a small lamp that she recognized as the one that blinded her during one of her brief moments of awareness. The light was now dim and manageable. Stretching her stiff limbs, she stood from the bed that had been her prison and teetered on unsteady legs.

"It would be best if you sat, my dear," a woman's voice drifted from the fog around her.

Nora took the advice and perched on the edge of what appeared to be a hospital bed, "Hello? Who's there?" she asked with a hoarse voice.

The thick, misty air swirled around her, and the smell of cigarettes invaded her nose. Pearl stepped forward into view with a gentle smile.

Nora was so glad to see a friendly face, "Pearl? Where are we?"

Pearl took a moment to look around at the space around them, "We're everywhere and nowhere, right now, dear. More specifically, I suppose we're in your mind," she tapped her own head with a giggle, "I'm so glad to see you, Nora. You gave us such a fright."

Everywhere and nowhere was not the answer that she was looking for. It was better than being told she was dead. She rubbed her weak fingers together and then up her arm, telling herself she was still whole. She was still alive, even if she only existed within her head, "So, am I dreaming?"

"Yes, dear. You're dreaming, but the difference is I'm actually here with you," Pearl moved to her side and sat, "Everyone has been so worried about you."

Nora held up a hand to silence her, wanting to know more about what was happening. If she was indeed still alive, she needed to know how to wake herself up, "How are you in my dream? I'm not imagining you?"

"Not the first question I thought you'd have, but one of the easiest to answer, so I'll take it. Let me officially introduce myself to you," Pearl smiled and held out her small, wrinkled hand, "Pearl Pitty, *Exspiravit Extraordinaire*."

Nora took her hand and shook it slightly, confused, "Expi-what?"

"*Exspiravit*, dear," Pearl laughed, "I'm a ghost. A spirit from beyond. OoooOOoooOOooo," she howled with the mock horror of a ghost's cry.

Having Pearl confirm that she was a ghost took Nora a few paces back from believing that she was still alive, "Am I dead? I mean... Am I a ghost now, too?"

"Yes and no," Pearl said, weighing her words, "You were dead. That's how I can be here now; you were dead a few times, actually," she frowned and nodded her head as she spoke, "It really has been quite a few days of excitement!" she exclaimed and started to dig through her purse, retrieving her cigarette case and a brass lighter, "You're not a ghost though. You're not dead enough for that. Well, not yet."

Nora stared back at the translucent woman, waiting for her to go on. She lit up without another word and sighed, lost in a thought she did not share.

"Not yet? What does that even mean? Am I dying?" Nora knew full well that the state of her body when she was conscious was not healthy in any way, and she could feel herself letting go a little more each time.

"Everyone dies, dear. That's the curse of life," she advised between long pulls on her cigarette, "As you are right now, you're not gone to us, and that's what we'll focus on. What you went through, my goodness, I can't believe how strong you've been. You're a very brave young lady."

"What about Ezra? And Jenny and the girls? Are they okay? They weren't hurt, were they? I heard Ezra and Jenny's voices. They're all okay, right?" Nora wouldn't be able to bear it if Quinn had harmed them.

"Yes, dear. They're all fine and safe. Don't fret for another moment for them. Not a hair on their heads was touched," Pearl said plainly and continued to puff away without another word.

"And Quinn?" she asked, already knowing the answer in her heart. She needed to hear someone say it. Even after all she had done, Nora could speak the words.

"Yes, dear. She's dead and gone now—ashes in the wind. I know you were close, and that must hurt, but it was for the best. She wasn't the woman you knew anymore, and she would have never stopped trying to put her hurt on everyone else. Some people are just broken, unfortunately," Pearl concluded.

There was relief that settled over her that Nora did not expect. It was true that Quinn was no longer her Aunt Quinn and had not been for quite some time. She had been grieving the loss of her since the day she saw her fangs. The woman that died in her apartment was a monster and nothing more.

"Am I going to turn into her now? I mean, the blood she made me drink. Will that make me like she was?" Nora asked, trying not to imagine becoming as cold, cruel, and vengeful as Quinn had become. Pearl only shrugged and puffed on her cigarette. Nora became frustrated and pushed when the silence continued, "So, what am I, then?"

"That's one of the tough questions," she shrugged, "We're not quite sure."

Nora remembered the fangs that had pierced her tongue. Her hands lightly touched the pointed razors that now protruded from her gums, "Am I a vampire?"

"That's what we're calling the best option right now," she chuckled, "It's better than some of the others. Especially dead and gone for good."

Being a vampire was not the best-case scenario, in Nora's opinion. When one of the options was final death, being turned vampire did not seem so bad. Unless it meant staying in the agonizing stasis that she had been left in. The more she remained in the moment with Pearl, the more dread she felt about returning to her body.

"Is this how I'm going to be forever? In some kind of painful coma," Nora asked, wondering if the fae blood mixed with the maker's would leave her in that desperate state forever, "Because I can't go on like this, Pearl. I can't."

Pearl flicked her half-finished cigarette into the milky fog and strung her arm through Nora's, "Oh, I know, sweetheart. You've been suffering so, so much. You can get through this. You're tougher than you think, and you must remember that you are not alone. You have a lot of people that care for you," she squeezed Nora's arm, "I've been with you from the beginning, you know. I've watched how strong you've been."

"That was you, wasn't it? In my apartment?" The mist that filled the room looked much like what had appeared in her room. Worrying that it could be made up of a multitude of spirits, she shifted further back onto the bed. It was creepy to think of them swimming around her, unseen.

Pearl dug around in her purse again, "Yes, I'd pop in to check on you from time to time. I couldn't leave Norman to do all the work."

"Norman!" Nora exclaimed, recalling the sight of him and his massive black feathers, "I saw him there. He had wings. I heard someone say there was an angel! Is that what he is? Is Norman an angel? A real live angel?"

"Yes, he certainly is. A virtue angel, to be precise. He has been here for a very long time. A sort of go-between for here and..." Pearl pointed her finger upwards, "Poor thing has had a nice quiet life for centuries before this mess. But that's why they're here, right? Nip problems in the bud before the whole universe is destroyed and such."

"Wow," Nora said through a breath. Norman, her reclusive, shut-in neighbor, was an angel on earth. He could indeed be called one when he saved her life. Well, he saved what was left of her life now that she was whatever she was.

Pearl watched her while the reality of all she had presented to her sunk in, "More importantly, the reason I'm here, dear, is to prepare you for what's next. Your heart is beating in your body right now, and I can tell it's getting tired from the fight. Once it stops, I can't come to you like this again. The moment it stops is when we will know your future. We will either lose you to the other side, or you will awaken vampire. Either way, your mortal human spirit is gone. Do you understand?"

Nora considered the two fates, neither being a choice she would make. Ezra had once said he would rather be dead than be a vampire. In her shoes, his preference would be easy to decide if it had been before Adalyn appeared. As it stood now, he had been reunited with his daughter, who was now precisely what he had vowed to kill. He could not feel the same now that he had her back in his life. Nora, on the other hand, was not his family. He may not be as forgiving of what she would become, and there was a chance he would turn his back on her. She would be all alone again after such a short time of feeling a sense of belonging. At least if she was turned, she could have time to decide if death would truly be better.

An ache started in her chest. The peaceful feeling of letting go when Quinn held her life in her hands was gone. In its place, she was panicked. She didn't want to die, no matter the way she would have to live. It was only a matter of time to find out what the universe would choose for her. There didn't seem to be anything she could do to push the odds one way or the other. The ache sharpened, clamping onto her heart, and she held a hand to her chest.

"Pearl, I…" Nora stopped when she saw she was alone. The only thing remaining of the kind woman was a slight smell of smoke in the air. The fog pushed onto her heavily until she was lying flat back on the bed. The pressure centered on her chest, entangling with the ripping pain in her heart and darkening as it swallowed her. Her mouth gaped, trying to pull in a breath that was being crushed out of her. The fog thickened until it was left as a blinding white light that overtook everything it could reach. Nora could feel it penetrating her body, lifting her up into its center. The grip on her heart dissipated and released her. She floated motionless in the gentle illumination.

The room was silent but for the heavy beat of her heart that loudly thumped in her ears, slowing with each pump.

Thump, thump...thump...thump...

Seconds went by without a sound, then minutes. Nora could not move. She could not speak or feel a thing around her as she floated inside her body, powerless. If this was death, she waited for her consciousness to cease, hoping that this would not be her forever. The calm that had overtaken her could not fight away the fear that started to build. The fear became anger. If only she had never followed Quinn. If only she had found the courage to strike out on her own. If only she had taken her life into her own hands when she had the chance, she would not have ended up with so many regrets. She might not have found herself ending so soon.

The soft sound of crying drifted into the space around her, and she felt her back touch down on the comfortable surface of the bed below. She could feel everything around her and hear the tiniest of sounds in the room—the slightest shift of the warm air on her chilled skin, the hum of the lightbulb beside her.

The bed when someone sat beside her. A shiver tickled her body when a tiny hand wrapped around hers. She gripped back when she felt a tight squeeze. The crying stopped.

"It's ok, daddy. She's here. She came back."

CHAPTER EIGHTEEN

XII
THE HANGED MAN.

Her eyes opened willingly as they did when she was with Pearl. The light from the small lamp was too bright, and she knew that meant she was back in the room where she had been comatose. She blinked the fuzzy shapes around her into focus, following a motion at her side. A floral silk scarf was placed over the lampshade, making the room easier on her eyes. The light below made the flowers on the fabric look as if they were glowing. Her nose twitched when she could smell the scent of detergent on the scarf as it warmed. The scent was followed by a rush of aromas of everything and everyone in the room. Her head spun, and her stomach turned until her brain could process the bouquet. She rubbed her eyes, trying to sit up. Ezra sat awestruck to one side of her, and his daughter Adalyn stood grinning on the other. He looked washed with exhaustion; his hair was mussed, and his face was shadowed with stubble.

The little girl fussed with the fabric she had placed over the harsh light and called out, "Gabriel! Get in here! She's awake!"

Nora pushed herself to sit up from the large bed she was in, tugging off the plush fur blankets tucked around her. That was not the medical-grade bed her imagination had her in when she found herself with Pearl. The room was nothing like she had pictured, and it certainly wasn't her apartment. The stone walls had the look of an ancient castle, and the luxe gold and crystal chandelier above her did the same. Looking down, she was dressed in silk pajamas that were much too big for her, the sleeves rolled up at her wrists.

"Where am I?" she asked Ezra as a medieval-looking door flew open across the expansive room.

Gabriel rushed in and moved at top speed to jump on the bed beside her, "You're at my place! Isn't it fabulous?" When he jostled her, Nora grimaced at the ache in her joints, "You're my roomie now, Nora. Emo-zra is gonna have to find someone else to mooch off of."

Nora took in the sight of him in his usual matching silk pajamas and robe that he would wear at the office. They were an exact match to the ones she was wearing. Gabriel grinned broadly when he saw that she had noticed his personal touch.

Nora started to speak again and stopped when she felt her fang against her tongue. It was real. She had been turned, "What do you mean your place? Where are we? How did we get here?"

"Could you give us a moment?" Gabriel asked, bobbing his head to the door, "We need to have a chat."

Ezra gave Nora's hand a squeeze, relief loosening his tense shoulders before he held a hand out for Adalyn to take, "We'll be right back, okay Nor?"

She nodded and rubbed at her gums. The sharp fangs had left the delicate skin around them feeling raw. Her eyes flashed to Ezra when he stood. Every slight motion of his body gave off a delicious smell that nearly caused Nora to drool. Her stomach rumbled loudly, and an ache started to spread. She turned to Gabriel, terrified that the pain which had crippled her was returning.

He turned to Ezra, "Why don't you go and get your little one a snack? They'll fix you up out there. Tell them that Nora is going to need one soon, as well," he directed and swung his long legs up to stretch out beside Nora when the door closed behind Ezra and Adalyn, "How's my little baby vamp doing? How are you feeling? Talk to me, girl."

"The pain is coming back," she faltered, realizing that it was no longer as severe, "It was coming back. Is that going to keep happening?"

"No, don't worry about that. You're just hungry. You know I have you covered there," he gave her a wink, "Whatever that was before looked way worse than being hungry."

"I didn't know that pain like that was even possible," she pulled the heavy fur blanket up to comfort her, "I can't believe I survived that. Well, didn't die, you know, completely."

"It was touch and go for a bit there, but I knew you'd pull through. That sassy little spitfire that I love was still in you," he tilted his head, silently looking her over, "How about now? How do you feel other than the hunger pains?"

Nora did a silent inventory of herself. Other than profound fatigue and a stiff body, she felt good. The torturous pain that had gripped her was gone without a trace, leaving only the tiny stomach grumbles that called out for a particular type of food she wasn't ready to admit to, "Pretty good, actually. Considering."

"I'm glad to hear it. You gave us quite the fright. You were being quite the drama queen for a bit there,' Gabriel tittered before his face tightened, "I really am glad that you're okay."

Okay was not what she would refer to herself as. Her tongue compulsively moved over her fangs until the skin split. It healed itself before she could even swallow the tiny bead of blood that had escaped. In the quiet of the room, her ears could pick up the voices of others moving about in other parts of wherever she found herself. She was caught off guard when she could pick up four distinctly different heartbeats as if her ear were to their chests. Her mouth watered.

"Whoa," she gulped, "That's too weird."

Gabriel smiled slyly, knowing what she was listening to, "Pretty cool, right? Oh, the things I will teach you! We're going to have so much fun together."

Nora looked around the room curiously. The windowless room should seem dank, yet the eclectic décor had been done in an elegant way that made it feel warm and homey. Just the thought of bright windows brought discomfort to her head. The light of the covered light was difficult enough to deal with, although her eyes were gradually adjusting. Her stomach rumbled again, and her body grew tired quickly.

"So, what now?" she asked, laying back against the mountain of pillows that were piled against the polished, carved headboard.

Gabriel sat up, and a severe look took the place of his amusement for a brief second, "Well, now we're going to keep you here for a bit to make sure you're completely okay, and then who knows?" he shrugged.

Nora watched him press a smile and then looked about the room again, "And where is here? This is your house?"

Gabriel waved his arm about him with a flourish, "We are currently in Mystique, in my private quarters."

"The nightclub?" Nora couldn't believe that a room that looked straight out of a royal fairy tale castle could be in the same building as the mirrored, bass-thumping bar that she had watched Dirt-Bag Derek being used as a feed bag. She was unsettled when that thought made her hungry, not disgusted. A shiver of revulsion tickled up her back.

"Yes, ma'am. One of my little hideaways that I enjoy," he bragged, "One of my favorites, in fact. Even more so now that you'll be spending time here."

Nora closed her eyes and dipped her head low, " Spending time here or locked down here like we were at Dunhope?" Nora scowled at him when he did not answer, "Why do I need to be here, Gabriel?"

He sighed and ran his fingers along the crease of his silk pajama pants, gathering his thoughts, "Let's just say, even with Quinn gone, there are a few, let's call them, *complications.*"

Of course, there were. Nora groaned loudly and pulled a pillow over her face. It wasn't enough that she was an undead bloodsucker; she was still being locked away from the world.

Out of the pot and into the fire.

Knowing she was a vampire now, she accepted the fact that she would never have the joy of seeing the light of day again. She had not considered that she would still be in danger.

"They're still out to get me? After all of this, there are still crazies that believe in Jude and Quinn?" she spat, exasperated by the unending nightmare her aunt had created for her.

"No, that's not it, deary," he pulled the pillow away from her face and tucked it under his arm, "This time, you're the complication."

Nora sat up, her head spinning with the incredible speed she had managed to move with, "Me? How am I the problem? Jude was turning people left and right, and they weren't locked away. What did I do?"

The murmurs of the far-off voices drifted into the room when Gabriel sat quietly nodding his head, trying to find the words to explain the new situation they found themselves in, "Jude was turning people with his own blood, Nora. Not the blood of the maker and not anyone that had fae blood floating around inside of them."

"So? I didn't do any of that! What the hell does that have to do with me?" Nora demanded. She was not going to go with the flow any longer. After losing her freedom, her sense of security, and then her actual heartbeat, there was no way she would take whatever was thrown at her lying down. When Gabriel said he had missed his little spitfire, he had no idea how much fire she had returned with. Each minute that passed had her feeling stronger and more alert. She would see to it that she had a say in any more changes that were to come.

"It's not that you did anything. None of this is your fault," Gabriel consoled as best as he could attempt, "What the problem is, is what you are," his mouth creased down, "What I mean is, your transition was difficult, to say the least. Your body was rejecting the blood we gave you, and we did almost lose you, Nora. It wasn't until we mixed in a few drops of fae blood that your body would accept it."

Nora narrowed her eyes at him, "I thought those two mixed would kill you instantly?" she questioned. If they were worried that a drop mixed would kill her, how could it do the opposite? She sat quietly, trying to understand how she was still on the right side of the soil.

Gabriel continued, spurred on by her waning anger, "Exactly. We're not sure why that worked. That's one of the reasons why we need to keep you here. We need to figure it all out."

Figuring out what happened to her and what *would* happen to her seemed to have a more evident end date than the constant unknown threat of Quinn floating around. If it was difficult to keep her alive, it could be sooner rather than later.

"Am I going to live?"

Gabriel put a hand lightly on her leg, his eyes fixed on a spot on the blanket, avoiding her gaze, "We don't know. It's more complicated than a yes or no answer."

"What can be done?"

Gabriel met her eyes and pushed on his signature happy bluster, "As far as we can tell, you're going to be happily un-dead for a long time. We have a plan, and we're going to do everything we can to keep you around. That's the other reason you're here," he added, "To get you fed and healthy, we think you'll need to keep having fae blood added to your meals. That being said, I think you know how they feel about giving up their blood and how they feel about vampires."

The idea of drinking the blood of any kind made her queasy, "What am I supposed to do then? How am I supposed to get it?"

A knock on the door as it opened grabbed their attention. Norman stood quietly watching them, looking as meek as always, his wings nowhere to be found.

Gabriel jumped from the bed to welcome him in, "This fellow here is turning into your very own guardian angel, girl! This is the good news that we can give you."

Norman took a step into the room, "Hello, Nora. How are you feeling?"

"Better than I'd expect for technically being dead," Nora mused and gave him a small smile, "Thank you for helping me," she added. It was more than help to save someone's life, but Nora didn't know how to thank an angel for killing her vampire aunt, who was in the midst of a murderous rage. The world had reached an all-time high of insanity. She hoped she was at the peak of it.

"All in a day's work," Norman replied with a shy grin of his own. He took a few more steps in when pushed along by Gabriel.

"Norman here has worked up a deal to get you fae blood on the sly. It has to be kept hush-hush, of course. That's why you'll be here," he exclaimed, giving the angel a slap on the shoulder that startled him into taking a step back.

"I appreciate you going out of your way for me, Norman. I can't thank you enough, but I have to ask. Will my life be nothing more than being locked up down here drinking stolen fae blood?" Nora slipped her legs from the bed, a sudden need to escape, to run from that future overtaking her. That was not a forever that she was willing to live as an immortal, "I'm not going to do that, Gabriel."

Norman held up his hands in peace and gestured for her to sit again, "It's not stolen, Nora, and you won't be here forever. It will just take time to sort things out. We need to learn as much as we can about you before letting the others know what has happened. We need to know exactly what will become of you before we present you to the world. It's the only way to keep you alive, Nora. Either you starve to death, or there is a good chance that the council will sentence you to death. That's what we're working with right now."

Gabriel seethed and interjected, "Those fucking council members do not like change. Especially deviations from what they deem normal."

Nora stayed seated but kept her feet on the ground, not entirely sure if she may still need to run. "Why would you do that for me? Why would you protect me?" she knew it would be easier to turn her over. She didn't understand why they were being so loyal to her when she had known them for such a short amount of time.

"We do need something from you in exchange," Norman stipulated, walking to the middle of the room, "Adalyn."

"What about her?" Nora asked quickly, "You're not going to hurt her, are you?" Nora would not let her life continue for the cost of that child. Adalyn was finally back with her father, and she would have no part in tearing them apart again. It would be better to stand before the council and have them do as they wish.

Norman shook his head quickly, "No, quite the opposite. Turning a child is the most despicable, blasphemous action in the eyes of all of us. It is cruel, and as such, it is completely banned. It is truly unthinkable. The problem we're facing is that when the council finds a child that has been turned, they are *disposed* of without a second thought," Norman stopped, unable to look up from the floor in front of him. He loudly cleared his throat before he continued, "I will not allow that to happen. We are not to meddle in council affairs unless it's requested, but I will not let them harm that little girl."

"How could they do that? How could they be so evil?" Nora raged. An innocent child having their life taken from them twice was more than Nora could bear. First, the violence of being turned and then executed for it? The council was sounding more and more like the real problem. Nora stilled, remembering Jude's same opinion. Being on his side of the fence had to be wrong.

"Evil has nothing to do with it, even though it does seem that way. It's about order," Norman answered and squared his shoulders, "It's about keeping a balance in the world. A child cannot handle the burdens and responsibilities that come hand in hand with the gift of immortality. Most children that is."

"But that's where you come in," Gabriel interrupted, "In exchange for your fairy juice, you're going to look after Adalyn. Here, in my home."

Nora could only look between them, her eyes blinking quickly as she tried to process what they were asking of her, "You're going to keep a little girl locked up here? With me? You can't expect her to live under a nightclub! And I'm not a parent. I don't know how to take care of a kid. Let alone a kid vampire. I don't know how to be a vampire, myself!"

Gabriel plopped on the bed beside her with an impish sparkle in his eyes, "Technically, you're still an employee of the bureau, so just think about this as an assignment," he said, tapping at the ankh branding on her arm, "You take great care of the witch's little one. It can't be that different" he put his arm over her shoulder and pulled her in for a hug, "and it's not forever. Just until it's all sorted out."

It seemed cruel not to do everything she could to help Adalyn. If there was a way that they could keep her from suffering the fate of the child vampires before her, that was what she was going to do. She deserved a second chance at life with her father after so much loss and suffering.

"What about Ezra? Is he going to be stuck here, too?" she asked, knowing that he would have a hard time going along with that, even for his daughter.

"No, we need to keep up appearances so that he will continue on with his training," Norman replied, "He will be able to visit her. To visit you both until it can be made known that you and Adalyn are alive."

As he spoke the words, Adalyn came skipping in, a medical-grade blood bag in each of her teeny hands. She scrambled up onto the bed and held one out to Nora, "Here, I got you this. They put your medicine in this one."

Nora hesitantly reached out to accept it, "Thank you, Adalyn."

"Bottoms up, Nora!" Gabriel squealed and clapped his hands with childlike delight.

She looked at the deep crimson liquid that was warm in her hand. Instead of being reviled, her stomach called out for it, her tongue lapping at her fangs. There was an animalistic effect that the scent had on her senses. She wanted to fight against it and fall into the desire for it all at once. Tipping the bag to her lips, she put the small straw-like tube in her mouth and took a sip. The delicious flavor explosion overcame her again, and she greedily slurped it up, squeezing the last few drops out with her fist.

"I don't think I'll ever get used to seeing that," Ezra said, his face twisted comically as he walked into the room, "So gross."

"Daddy! Don't tease us," Adalyn giggled and jumped down to run to him. Ezra swept her up into his arms, a smile bursting across his face, "Thanks for saving my daddy from Papa Jude, Nora. I honest didn't know he was a bad man."

Nora didn't know how to respond and instead just smiled and watched the joy on Ezra's face.

"Well? Did they tell you the plan?" he asked.

Nora was surprised that he already knew and that his expectant tone sounded as if he was already on board.

"They did. You're okay with this?"

In the face of all that had happened, a relief had come over Ezra that Nora had never seen in him before. He glowed with happy contentment.

"What? Having my vampire daughter raised in the basement of a vampire nightclub? What could be more normal?" he asked with a laugh, "Whatever keeps her safe and close is what I'm going to do," he set her on the end of the bed and sat beside her, "And I guess it's pretty great that it keeps you here too," he added with a half grin.

Considering that Nora was currently an uncertain freak of a vampire and was now tasked with watching over Ezra's vampire daughter, along with his new assignment on the vampire hit crew, the world of Aumbry Valley had become a whole lot more complicated. At least she was finally out of Dunhope Manor. The future was uncertain, but at least they would not be facing it alone. What was said about Aumbry Valley was proving to be true. If the valley wanted you to stay, it would always find a way.

KATHERINE DEMPSTER

author